CHILDREN'S CLASSICS
EVERYMAN'S LIBRARY

Russian
Fairy Tales

Retold by Gillian Avery
with illustrations by Ivan Bilibin

EVERYMAN'S LIBRARY
CHILDREN'S CLASSICS
Alfred A. Knopf New York London Toronto

THIS IS A BORZOI BOOK
PUBLISHED BY ALFRED A. KNOPF

First included in Everyman's Library Children's Classics 1995
Design and typography © 1995 by Everyman's Library
Book design by Barbara de Wilde, Carol Devine Carson and Peter B. Willberg

Eleventh printing (US)

Illustrations to *The Tale of Tsar Saltan, Vassilissa the Beautiful, The Tale of Tsarevich Ivan, the Firebird and the Grey Wolf, Sister Alenushka and her Brother Ivanushka* and *The White Duck* reproduced by kind permission of the Opie Collection, Bodleian Library, Oxford. Illustrations to *Marya Morevna* and *The Frog Princess* reproduced by kind permission of the V & A Picture Library, Victoria and Albert Museum, London.

Five of Ernest H. Shepard's illustrations from *Dream Days* by Kenneth Grahame are reprinted on the endpapers by permission of The Bodley Head, London. The sixth illustration is by S. C. Hulme Beaman.

Prologue to *Russian and Lyudmila* by Alexander Pushkin, translated by Dimitri Obolensky. Reprinted from *The Penguin Book of Russian Verse*, Penguin Books, 1962. Copyright © Dimitri Obolensky, 1962, 1965.

www.randomhouse.com/everymans
www.everymanslibrary.co.uk

ISBN 978-0-679-43641-6 (US)
978-1-85715-935-6 (UK)

A CIP catalogue record for this book is available from the British Library

Library of Congress Cataloging-in-Publication Data

Avery, Gillian, 1926–
Russian fairy tales/retold by Gillian Avery; [illustrated by Ivan Bilibin].
p.   cm.—(Everyman's library children's classics)
Summary: An illustrated collection of traditional Russian tales including "Vassilissa the Beautiful," "The Frog Princess," and "The White Duck."
ISBN 978-0-679-43641-6
1. Fairy tales—Russian. 2. Tales—Russian. [1. Fairy tales.]
[2. Folklore—Russia.] I. Bilibin, Ivan Iakovlevich, 1876–1942, ill.
II. Title. III. Series.

PZ8.3.A9274Rn   1995   95-15334
398.2—dc20   CIP
                                                                     AC

Typeset in the UK by AccComputing, North Barrow, Somerset
Printed and bound in Germany by GGP Media GmbH, Pössneck

CONTENTS

PROLOGUE

By the shores of a bay there is a green oak tree; there is a golden chain on that oak; and day and night a learned cat ceaselessly walks round on the chain; as it moves to the right, it strikes up a song, as it moves to the left, it tells a story.

There are marvels there: the wood-sprite roams, a mermaid sits in the branches; there are tracks of strange animals on mysterious paths; a hut on hen's legs stands there, without windows or doors; forest and vale are full of visions; there at dawn the waves come washing over the sandy and deserted shore, and thirty fair knights come out one by one from the clear water, attended by their sea-tutor; a king's son, passing on his way, takes a dreaded king prisoner; there, in full view of the people, a sorcerer carries a knight through the clouds, across forests and seas; a princess pines away in prison, and a brown wolf serves her faithfully; a mortar with Baba Yaga the wicked witch in it walks along by itself. There the wicked King Kashchey grows sickly beside his gold; there is a Russian odour there – it smells of Russia! And I was there, I drank mead, I saw the green oak tree by the sea and sat under it, while the learned cat told me its stories. I remember one – and this story I will now reveal to the world ...

ALEXANDER PUSHKIN (1799–1837)

[Prologue to *Ruslan and Lyudmila*, trans. Dimitri Obolensky]

THE TALE OF TSAR SALTAN AND OF HIS SON THE TSAREVICH GUIDON

by Alexander Pushkin

ONCE upon a time three girls sat spinning by the window of their home. 'If I were Tsarina,' said one of them, who enjoyed cooking, 'I would make a feast for the whole world and his wife.' 'If I were Tsarina,' said the second, who was a skilled weaver, 'I'd weave linen cloth for them.' But the youngest said: 'If I were Tsarina I would want to bear the Tsar a son who was a hero.'

Scarcely had she said this when the door opened and the Tsar himself came into the room. He had been listening outside the shuttered window, and what the third sister had said had much moved him. 'Fair maiden,' he said, 'your wish is granted. You shall be my wife, and by the end of September you must bear me a son.' Then he spoke to the sisters. 'As for you, my little doves, you will be part of my household. The eldest will be my cook and the other must weave and sew.'

So the three sisters went to the Tsar's court, and that very night he ordered a wedding feast, much to the chagrin and envy of the other two sisters. After the banquet the Tsar and

his bride were led to an ivory bed, and that very night she conceived a son.

But the country was at war and the Tsar had to leave his young wife. He said farewell and told her to take good care of herself, and then he rode off with his troops. He was still far away when her child was born. She watched over it like a she-eagle over her eaglet, and proud of this marvellous baby, who at birth was already three feet tall, she at once sent a messenger to Tsar Saltan. But her sisters – the cook and the weaver – together with a marriage-broker called Babarikha plotted to bring about her downfall. They arranged for the messenger to be followed and captured, and in his place they sent another with the news that the queen had borne not a son or a daughter, nor even a mouse or a frog, but a monster.

When the Tsar heard this he was enraged and wanted to hang the courier. But he relented and sent back instructions that they must wait for his return before any decision should be taken about the child.

So the courier rode home. But the two sisters and Babar-ikha waylaid him, filled him with drink until he was tipsy, and then put another message in his wallet. This said that the Tsar ordered his boyars* to throw his young wife and the child into the sea. Much grieved, the boyars came to her room and read out the decree. But since it was the Tsar's command there was no help for it; the Tsarina and her infant son were put into a barrel, and the barrel was nailed up and cast off into the sea.

Under the glittering stars and the wandering clouds the barrel tossed on the sea and the waves splashed over it. The Tsarina wept and struggled, and all the time, hour by hour, the baby grew. He called to one of the waves: 'You are free and go where you want. You roll over the rocks, you flood the shores and bear the ships – have mercy on us, wash us on to the dry land!'

And the wave obeyed. Very gently the barrel was washed on the shore and the mother and the baby were safe. But how

*noblemen

were they going to get out of the barrel? The son rose to his feet, and braced himself against a stave with his head. 'How about breaking through this window?' he said. And he burst it and scrambled out.

Both mother and son were now free, but they were hungry. Up on a hill above the shore they saw an oak tree, and from this the son broke off a branch, bent it into a bow and strung a silken cord across it. Then he took a twig and shaped it into an arrow, and went back to the shore to look for game.

As he reached the sea he heard a cry, and saw a swan struggling in the waves. A kite was hovering above her, and she, trying to escape, was thrashing the water with her wings. But the bird of prey had spread his talons and was poised to strike with his blood-stained beak. Then the young prince's arrow whistled through the air and struck the kite in the neck. It dropped bleeding into the sea, where the swan pecked at it and beat at it with her wings until it disappeared below the water.

Then the swan spoke to the Tsarevich in Russian. 'You have come to my rescue,' she said. 'Do not grieve that after this you will not eat for three days; nor that your arrow was lost in the sea. You will find that this does not matter, for I will repay you. It was not a swan that you saved but a

И. БИЛИБИНЪ. 1905

maiden, and the kite that you killed was a sorcerer. I shall
serve you for the rest of your life. But now turn back, and lie
down and go to sleep.'

The swan flew off, and in spite of their empty stomachs,
the Tsarina and her son did as she said, and slept. But when
the Tsarevich woke next morning he was astonished, for
lying before him he saw a great city with battlemented walls
and behind them the domes of churches and monasteries. He
woke his mother and told her that the swan must have been
very busy.

They walked towards the city, and as they went through
the gateway they were greeted by a deafening peal of bells.
People thronged all round them, there was the sound of
singing, courtiers appeared in golden coaches and welcomed
them. And there and then the Tsarevich was crowned as the
ruler of the country, and began to reign that day under the
title of Duke Guidon.

Out at sea a little ship was passing, and the ship's company
clustered together and stared at the extraordinary sight. The
island that they knew was now transformed. There was a
golden-domed city above the shore, and a harbour from
which they could hear the sound of cannonfire – a signal for
them to drop anchor there. Duke Guidon himself greeted
them as his guests, plied them with food and drink, and said:
'You are merchants, I can see that, but what are you trading
in and where are you bound for?' And the sailors replied: 'We
have sailed all round the world, trading in furs – in sables,
black and russet fox skins. And now that our business is

finished we are sailing due east, past the island of Buyan, to the tsardom of Tsar Saltan.'

Then Duke Guidon said: 'A good passage to you, gentlemen, and greet Tsar Saltan for me.' As the traders put out to sea he watched them, grieving. The swan swam up and asked him what saddened him. 'I am sick to see my father,' said Duke Guidon. 'Well then,' said the swan, 'if you would like to fly to sea after the ship I will turn you into a gnat.' And she beat her wings, churned up the water and splashed him all over. Then he shrank to the size of a dot, became a gnat and shrilled after the ship. There, dropping down on to the deck he tucked himself into a crack.

And so the ship, with a following wind, sailed merrily on past the island of Buyan, to the land of Tsar Saltan. Once in the harbour the merchants went ashore. The Tsar bade them be his guests, and Duke Guidon the gnat flew after them. He saw his father Tsar Saltan, shining in gold, sitting on his throne in the chamber of state, with a sad expression on his face. And beside him were the cook and the weaver – Duke Guidon's aunts – together with the marriage-broker Babarikha.

The Tsar invited the merchants to sit at his table beside him and questioned them thus: 'Now gentlemen, tell me your news. Have you been journeying long? And what did you see beyond these shores? Did you come across any wonders?'

To this the sailors replied: 'We have traversed the whole world, and yes, we did see a wonderful sight. There is a

craggy island – we knew it of old, and remembered it as bare and uninhabited with just a single young oak tree growing on it. But now a new city stands there, with a palace and golden-domed churches, castles and gardens. Duke Guidon rules over it and he sent you his greetings.'

The Tsar marvelled and said: 'If I live long enough I shall visit this wonderful island.'

But the two sisters and Babarikha tried to distract him. 'A city by the sea!' said the cook contemptuously, with a sly wink at the others. 'I know something better than that. There is a spruce tree in a wood, and beneath it is a squirrel. The squirrel sings to itself and keeps gnawing little nuts. But these nuts are no ordinary ones – they have golden shells and the kernels are emeralds. This is what I call a marvel.'

The Tsar was impressed, but the gnat was full of anger and he bit the cook in her right eye. She went pale and stiff, and then doubled up with pain, and her sister together with Babarikha and the other servants chased the gnat with shrieks of fury. But he escaped through the window and flew back calmly to his own country.

There once again, in his own shape, the Duke walked by the shore and stared out to sea. And as before the swan came swimming up. 'Hail, Prince!' she said, 'why are you so subdued and dejected?'

'I am haunted by a story I have heard,' he told her. 'Somewhere there is a spruce tree in a wood, and beneath the tree there is a squirrel who sings and gnaws little nuts. But the nuts are not ordinary ones; the shells are golden and they have emeralds inside. But maybe there's no truth in the tale.'

'Dear Prince,' said the swan, 'there's no need to grieve any longer. I am glad to be able to help you in this little matter.'

So, with a lightened heart the Duke went home. And there in the big courtyard of his palace he saw a tall spruce and under it a little squirrel gnawing at a golden nut and taking from it an emerald. It gathered up the shell, added it to a neat pile, and sang and whistled to the onlookers: 'In the garden, in the orchard.'

The Duke was amazed: 'What a swan! God give her the same joy as I have been given!' Then he made a crystal enclosure for the squirrel and had it guarded, and appointed a clerk to keep a tally of the nuts. (Profit for the Duke, honour for the squirrel!)

Over the sea a little ship was running before the wind. As it passed the craggy island and the great city, cannons were fired from the pier commanding the vessel to put in. The merchants made their ship fast, and Duke Guidon welcomed them as his guests. After they had eaten he asked them to give an account of themselves: 'What are you trading in and where are you bound for?'

The sailors replied: 'We have gone right round the world. We traded in horses – ponies from the lands of the Don – and now our business is finished and we have a long haul home, past the island of Buyan to the land of the great Saltan.'

'A good passage to you then, gentlemen,' said the Duke, 'and greet the Tsar for me.'

The merchants bowed to the Duke, went out and got under way. And the Duke went back to the sea-shore. The swan was already there, and when she saw his look of sorrowful yearning she once again splashed him with water. This time he was changed into a fly. He flew off, dropped down on to the ship, and crawled into a crack.

The ship sped fast before the wind, past the island of Buyan, until the coast of the tsardom of Saltan was sighted. When their vessel was safely berthed the merchants went ashore, guests of the great Tsar himself, and behind them flew Duke Guidon, in the form of a fly. He saw the gold-clad Tsar sitting in state on his throne, but looking sad and distracted. Near him sat the cook and the weaver and Babar-ikha, staring like wicked toads.

The Tsar put the merchants next to him at his table and questioned them. 'Have you been at sea a long time? Where have you been, and how are things in the world at large? Have you seen any marvels?'

They replied: 'We have been round the world. Life at sea is fair enough, but we can tell you of a marvel. There is an island with a city on it, with gold-topped churches, and castles and gardens. In front of the palace there is a spruce tree and beneath it a crystal house. And in it lives a tame squirrel with extraordinary powers. He sings and gnaws nuts – not ordinary nuts but gold ones with emeralds inside. The army salutes him, and he has his own bodyguard, and a state clerk who keeps an account of the nuts. They mint coins out of the nutshells and put them in circulation all round the world. And girls store the emeralds in treasure-houses. Everyone on this island is rich; there aren't any cottages, only mansions.'

The Tsar was awestruck. 'If only I live long enough, I shall visit this island as Guidon's guest,' he said. But the cook and the weaver and Babarikha had no intention of letting him go there, and the weaver smiling slyly said: 'Well, what's so wonderful – even if it's true – about a squirrel sweeping up gold and raking emeralds into piles? I can tell you of something to beat that. Somewhere there's a place where a stormy sea surges up the shingle on an empty shore. A wave rolls up and thirty-three knights walk out in coats of mail glowing like fire. They are handsome, tall as giants, and all alike, and with them comes old Chernomor*. There's a real wonder for you!'

*A wizard who appears in many Russian fairy tales

The Tsar marvelled, but Guidon was enraged. He gave a buzz and landed on his aunt's left eye. She turned pale, gave a cry, and doubled up. Everybody round her gave chase and tried to swat the fly. But the Duke was off through the window and flew home across the sea.

*

Again Guidon was walking by the shore and staring out to sea. And over the waves came the swan. 'Are you grieved, fair Prince?' she asked. 'Why do you look so sad?'

'I am eaten up by longing,' he told her. 'There is a marvellous thing that I want for my own.'

'And what is that?' she said.

'There is a lonely shore beaten by stormy seas, where thirty-three heroes walk out from the waves. They are all identical, handsome young giants, and old Chernomor comes with them.'

'Is that all that troubles you, Prince?' said the swan. 'Think no more of it. These knights of the sea are all my own brothers. Do not fret any longer, but hurry back and wait for them.'

So the Duke went off reassured. He climbed the tower and looked out to sea. Suddenly the waves mounted and heaved and rushed up on the shore, and thirty-three knights strode out in coats of mail glowing like fire. They marched in pairs, and the silver-haired Chernomor led them to the city. Duke Guidon hurried down from the tower and went to greet them. Their leader said: 'The swan has sent us to you to guard your famous city. We shall come out of the sea every day without fail to patrol your walls. But now we must go back, we find the air of the earth stifling.'

*

Once more a little ship was being driven over the sea by the wind. It approached the craggy island, and cannons summoned it into the harbour. The sailors made it fast, and Duke Guidon invited them to be his guests. After they had eaten and drunk he questioned them. 'Well, my friends, what was your cargo, and where are you bound for?'

'We have sailed round the world,' the merchants told him, 'trading in Damascus steel, silver and gold. Now all that is over and we are on our way home, past the island of Buyan, to the tsardom of Saltan.' And the Duke wished them godspeed, and sent his greetings to the Tsar.

The merchants bowed and left, and the Duke followed them down to the shore. The swan was already there, and when she saw his yearning face she splashed him once more with water. Instantly he shrank and turned this time into a bee. He overtook the ship and, dropping down on to the stern, found a crack to hide in.

The wind drove the ship on, past the island of Buyan, and the shores of the tsardom came in sight. Saltan invited the merchants to the palace, and behind them flew the bee. He saw the Tsar on his throne, wearing his crown, and saw the sadness of his face. The cook and the weaver and Babarikha were near, eying him, but now there were only four eyes among the three of them. The Tsar placed the merchants near him at his table and questioned them about their trade and what they had seen. Had they encountered any wonder, he asked.

The merchants replied that there was one great wonder. 'It is on an island where a city stands. Daily the sea boils up, surges up the empty shore, breaks splashing on it and leaves there thirty-three knights in golden armour, tall, handsome young men. Old Chernomor comes out of the sea with them and marches them in pairs to guard the island – there is no guard that is braver or more reliable. Duke Guidon rules over this island and he sends you greetings.'

Tsar Saltan was deeply impressed. 'One day if I live I shall visit this island.' But Babarikha scoffed. 'What's so extraordinary about all this? Men coming out of the sea to keep watch! Whether it's true or a lie there's nothing very strange in that. Here is something that puts it in the shade. Beyond the sea there is a princess who outshines all other mortals. By day she dims the sun, by night lights up the earth. The moon gleams under her hair, and on her brow glows a star. She is splendid to look at, clad in peacock colours, and when she speaks it is like a brook murmuring. You can say with justice that this is a marvel.'

The merchants were silent, not wishing to argue with the woman, and the Tsar marvelled. But Duke Guidon, though he was angry, did not want to injure Babarikha's eyes, so he buzzed over to the old woman and stung her nose. A lump swelled up at once, and again there was consternation among the onlookers. 'Help, for God's sake! Catch him! Swat him!

We'll show you – hold on!' But the bee was already through the window and on his way to his own land.

The Duke went back to the shore, and the white swan came swimming towards him. 'What ails you, Prince?' she asked as usual. 'Why do you look so downcast?'

'I am consumed with sadness,' he told her. 'People marry. Only I am left.' 'But have you anyone in view?' she asked. 'They say,' said the Duke, 'that there is a princess who holds the eyes of all who see her. By day she dims the sun; by night she lights up the earth. The moon shines in her hair, and a star gleams on her forehead. She is splendid as a peacock to look at, and she speaks as sweetly and softly as a brook. Do you think all this is true?'

The swan was silent, then said: 'Yes, there is such a maiden. But a wife is not like a glove. You can't just shake her off your hand or tuck her behind your belt. Give it all some thought, so that you don't have regrets afterwards – this is my advice.'

The Duke started protesting. It was time for him to get married; he had thought about it for a long time. He was ready, heart and soul, and he would walk through three times nine lands to reach his princess. The swan sighed and said: 'Why should you go so far? Your destiny is much nearer – I myself am this princess.' Then, beating her wings, she flew up from the waves, and lighting on the shore among some bushes, turned into a princess. The moon was shining in her hair, and a star on her forehead. She bore herself nobly and when she spoke it was like a brook murmuring.

The Duke embraced her, led her to his mother, and said: 'Gracious mother, I have chosen a wife for myself, and an obedient daughter for you. We both ask your consent; bless your children that they may live in harmony and love.'

'God will reward you, my children,' said the mother with tears in her eyes.

So without delay the Duke and the princess swan were married, and settled down and awaited a child.

*

On the sea a little ship was running before the wind with bellying sails. As it passed the steep island crowned with the city, cannons fired from the pier signalled the ship to come in. It berthed, and Duke Guidon called the merchants up to the palace to be his guests. When they had eaten and drunk he asked them about their voyage. They told him that they had traded successfully, and that now after much wandering were on their way home to the land of Tsar Saltan.

Then the Duke said: 'I wish you well, gentlemen, on the

last lap of your journey. And remind your sovereign that he has always promised me a visit but so far has never come. Greet him for me.'

The merchants departed, but this time Duke Guidon stayed at home with his wife.

The wind was fair, and the little ship sped before it, and the familiar coasts of Tsar Saltan's land came in sight. The merchants went ashore, and were invited up to the palace. There they found the Tsar sitting, watched by the cook, the weaver, and Babarikha (four eyes among the three of them, and one with a lump on her nose). He asked the merchants about their voyage, and whether they had seen anything of particular note. Then they told him about the marvellous island with its city and gold-topped buildings; about the spruce tree under which a squirrel in a crystal house was for

ever gnawing at golden nuts with emeralds inside; about the thirty-three knights headed by old Chernomor who daily came out of the sea to patrol the city. 'And,' they ended, 'the Duke has a young wife and we could not take our eyes off her. She outshines the sun by day, and lights up the earth at night. The moon seems to shine in her hair, and there is a star on her brow. Duke Guidon rules that city, and everyone sings his praise. He sends you greetings, but laments that you have never paid him the visit you have promised.'

Then the Tsar could bear no more, and commanded that his fleet should be made ready. The two sisters – the cook and the weaver – and Babarikha the marriage-broker, tried to stop him, but this time the Tsar would not listen. 'I am not a child!' he said furiously, stamping his foot, and went out slamming the door.

*

Duke Guidon sat by the window, staring out at the sea. It was very calm and still. Then, over the horizon, ships became visible, Tsar Saltan's fleet. The Duke stood up and shouted for his mother and his young wife. 'Look!' he cried. 'My father is coming!'

The fleet was nearing the island, and as the Duke put his glass to his eye he could see the Tsar on deck doing the same. And beside him stood the cook and the weaver and Babarikha, all of them astonished at this new country.

On the land they started firing cannons, ringing the bells, and the Duke put off in a boat to welcome the Tsar, the cook and the weaver, and Babarikha. Then once on shore again he led the Tsar to the palace.

They went through the gleaming gates towards the state apartments. Outside stood the Tsar's bodyguard – thirty-three handsome knights all alike, and old Chernomor with them. And there in the courtyard, below a spruce, a squirrel was singing a little song as he nibbled at a golden nut, took out an emerald and dropped it into a bag – the yard being strewn with golden shells. And look! The Duke's young wife with the moon in her hair and a star on her brow, striding out stately as a peacock and leading her mother-in-law!

The Tsar gazed and his heart leapt. 'What do I see? Who is this?' And he wept and took the Queen, his own dear wife, into his arms, then embraced his son and his daughter-in-law.

Then there was a great feast, but the two sisters (the cook and the weaver) and Babarikha fled, and it was some time before they could be found. They confessed what they had done and admitted their guilt. But the Tsar was so happy that he forgave them and sent them home. And the day went by with much feasting and drinking – the Tsar had to be carried to bed at the end of it. I was there, but the beer and the mead only wetted my whiskers.

VASSILISSA THE BEAUTIFUL AND THE WITCH BABA YAGA

FAR away and long ago there once lived a merchant. He had been married for twelve years but he had only one child, a daughter, who from her earliest days had been called Vassilissa the Beautiful. When the little girl was eight her mother became ill, and realized that she had not long to live. So she called the child to her, and giving her a tiny wooden doll, said to her: 'I am dying, little Vassilissa, and I leave you this doll with my blessing. It is very precious, and there is no other doll like it anywhere. Put it in your pocket, always have it with you, and never show it to anyone. But if ever you are in trouble or sorrow, go into a corner, take it out, give it something to eat and drink; after that you can ask for help and it will advise you.' Then she kissed her little daughter, blessed her, and soon afterwards she was dead.

That night little Vassilissa could not sleep for crying. At last she thought of the doll, and took it from the pocket of her dress. She found a piece of bread and a cup of *kwas**, put them in front of the doll, and said: 'Dear doll, eat and drink a little of this. I shall never see my mother again and I am so lonely and sad.'

Then the doll's eyes began to shine like fireflies and it ate a crumb of bread and took a sip of *kwas*. Then it said: 'Don't cry, little Vassilissa. Grief is worse at night. Lie down and go to sleep. The morning is wiser than the evening.' So Vassilissa went back to bed, and sure enough she felt better when she woke.

The merchant mourned for his wife as was only right, but he soon began to wish to marry again. He was a wealthy man, and a good one too who gave much money to the poor, so there were plenty of people to choose from, and after he had considered the matter carefully he decided to take as his second wife a widow with two daughters. She, he thought, would not only be a good housekeeper, but would be a kind stepmother to his own little daughter.

But she was a cold, cruel, designing woman who had only married the merchant for his wealth. Her own daughters were as ugly as two crows, whereas Vassilissa was the great-

*beer

est beauty in the village. All three therefore envied and hated her. They tried to humiliate her in every way, and gave her menial tasks to do in the hope that the work would coarsen her and make her ugly. She submitted without complaint, and the fact was that while her stepmother's daughters always grew plainer in spite of the easy life they led, little Vassilissa every day became more radiant and beautiful.

The secret of this was the doll. Without her help Vassilissa could never have got through the heavy work. But every night when the household was asleep she would take the doll into a closet, give it a little to eat and drink, and then tell it her troubles, and of the latest task she had been set. And the doll would not only comfort her, but while she slept would do all her work itself. The garden would be weeded, the cabbage beds watered, water fetched from the well, wood chopped for the stoves. So Vassilissa's hands stayed white and smooth and her face never became rough and brown from the wind and the sun.

Time went on and Vassilissa became old enough to marry. All the young men in the village courted her, but not one of them would look at her stepmother's ugly daughters. This made their mother even angrier. She told the suitors that never could the youngest girl be married before the two older ones, and she took to beating Vassilissa, who would have been wretched indeed if it had not been for her doll.

Now there came a time when the merchant was obliged to travel to a distant tsardom. He said farewell to his wife and her two daughters, kissed Vassilissa and blessed her, and told her to pray for his safe return. As soon as he had left, his wife sold the house, and removed herself and the three girls to a distant place on the edge of a huge dark forest. As she knew very well, a terrible Baba Yaga, the grandmother of all witches, lived in this forest, in a wretched hut on hen's legs. She ate humans as people eat chickens, and every day the merchant's wife sent Vassilissa into the forest on some errand or other, hoping that the girl would never come back. But she was always safe, because the doll told her where to find the berries or the mushrooms she had been ordered to fetch, and it took care to keep her away from the hut on hen's legs.

So the stepmother had to devise a new plan. One autumn evening she called the three girls to her and set each of them a task. She told one of her daughters to make a piece of lace, the other to knit a pair of stockings, and she gave Vassilissa a basket of flax to spin. Then she put out all the fires in the house, and left just a single candle in the room where the girls were working.

They went on with their allotted tasks, and then one of the girls took up the tongs to straighten the wick of the candle. Acting on her mother's orders, she put the candle out, as if by accident. She pretended to be much alarmed. 'There's only one thing, for it,' she said. 'Someone will have to go and fetch fire. There's no other light in the house, and we haven't nearly finished our work.'

'There's no one who lives anywhere near,' said the other. 'Only the Baba Yaga in the forest. I'm not going there. Anyway, I can see enough to do my lace from the steel pins.'

'And I can see enough for my knitting from the silver needles,' said the first. 'So Vassilissa will have to fetch the light. She can't possibly see enough to do her spinning.'

Both girls got up, pushed Vassilissa out of the house and slammed the door, saying: 'You're not coming back in unless you bring back a flame to light the candle.'

Poor Vassilissa sat down on the doorstep. But she had her doll in her pocket, and some bits of supper. She put the food in front of the doll and said: 'Dear doll, eat and then listen to my sorrow. I have been sent to the Baba Yaga's hut in the forest to ask for fire and I am afraid she will eat me. What shall I do?'

Then the doll's eyes shone like two stars and it became alive. 'Do not be afraid, Vassilissa,' it said. 'Go where you have been sent. The old witch can't do you any harm while I am with you.' So Vassilissa put the doll back in her pocket, crossed herself, and started out.

She stumbled on through the dark, full of fear. Then suddenly she heard the sound of a horse's hooves and a mounted knight galloped past her. He was dressed all in white; the horse he rode was milk-white and the harness was white, and as he passed her she could see through the branches of the trees that the sky was getting lighter.

She went a little further and then again there was the sound of a horse. This time a rider dressed all in red came galloping through the forest. His horse was blood-red with a red harness, and just as he passed her the sun rose.

Vassilissa walked all day. By this time she had completely

lost her way and she could not call on the doll for help for she
had no food to make it come alive. But as the light was fading
and evening was approaching she came into a clearing of the
forest. There stood a tumbledown hut on hen's legs which
was spinning round and round, and she knew she had
reached the Baba Yaga's house. The fence round the hut was
made of human bones and on its top were skulls. There was a
gate with hinges made of the bones of human feet, and locks
made of jaw-bones set with teeth. Vassilissa stood there,
frozen with horror.

Then behind her a third man came galloping through the
trees. His face was black, he was dressed in black, and he rode
a coal-black horse. He went up to the gate and there he
disappeared as if he had sunk into the ground. At this
moment night came on and the forest became dark. Immediately the eyes of the skulls on the fence lit up and the clearing
became as bright as day.

As Vassilissa stood trembling the forest became full of a
fearful noise; the trees began to creak and groan, and the
leaves underfoot heaved and rustled. Then the Baba Yaga
came flying through the wood. She was riding in a great iron
mortar, driving it with a pestle, and sweeping away her trail
behind her with a kitchen broom. She rode up to the gate and
said:

> 'Little house, little house,
> Stand the way your mother placed you,
> Turn your back to the forest,
> Turn your face to me.'

And the little hut turned to face her, and stood still. Then the Baba Yaga snuffed with her long nose and said: 'Fee, fi, fo, fum. I can smell Russian blood. Who is there?'

Vassilissa, very frightened, came out of the shadows, bowed low in front of her and said: 'It is only me, grandmother. My stepmother's daughters sent me to borrow some fire.'

'I know them well enough,' said the Baba Yaga grimly. 'Well, I'll give you fire on one condition. You've got to stay with me for a bit and work. If you don't I'll eat you.' Then she shouted to the gates to open. They obeyed, and when she and Vassilissa were inside they slammed shut.

Inside the hut, the Baba Yaga threw herself down on the stove, stretched out her bony legs and said: 'Get to work, won't you – can't you see I'm hungry? Take the food from the oven and put it on the table.'

So Vassilissa lit a splinter of wood from the glowing eyes of one of the skulls on the wall, and ran to the oven. There was enough meat there for three strong men. Then she fetched *kwas* and mead and wine from the cellar, and the Baba Yaga gobbled and gorged until everything had gone except a little cabbage soup and a crust of bread, which was Vassilissa's share. She stretched herself on the stove again and said: 'Now listen to me. Tomorrow after I have left you have got to clean the yard, sweep the floors and cook my supper. That ought not to take you long, so go to my store room, take a sack of millet and pick out all the black grains and the wild peas. And if I find anything is left unfinished I shall eat you for my supper.'

Then the Baba Yaga turned her face to the wall and began to snore. Poor Vassilissa crept into a corner of the room, took the doll from her pocket and put a morsel of cabbage soup and a crumb of bread in front of it. 'Eat and drink, dear little doll,' she said, 'for please, I need your help. I cannot possibly do the things the old witch has ordered, and she is going to eat me.'

Then the eyes of the doll began to glow like two candles. It ate a little of the soup and the bread and said: 'Don't be afraid, Vassilissa. Say your prayers and go to sleep. The morning is wiser than the evening.' Vassilissa was comforted. She said her prayers, lay down on the floor and was soon fast asleep.

When she woke next morning it was still dark. She got up and peered through the window, and she saw that the eyes of the skulls were growing dim. While she stood there, the man in white riding a white horse came galloping round the hut. He leapt over the fence, and as he disappeared it became quite light, and the eyes of the skulls flickered and went out. The old witch was in the yard. She gave a shrill whistle and the great iron mortar and pestle and the broom flew out of the hut to her. As she got into the mortar the man dressed in red, on a blood-red horse, came round the corner of the hut, leapt over the fence and was gone. At that instant the sun rose, and the Baba Yaga shrieked: 'Ho, my solid locks, unlock! And you strong gates, open!' And the locks unlocked and the gates opened and she was off, driving the mortar with her pestle, and sweeping her tracks away with the broom.

Vassilissa, left alone, looked round and wondered where

she ought to begin with her tasks. But now there was daylight she could see there was nothing left to be done. The floors of the hut were swept, the yard was neat and clean, and when she went to the store room the doll was already there, picking out the last black grains and peas from the millet. 'Go and cook the Baba Yaga's supper,' it said to her. 'That is all that is left for you to do.' And it crept back into her pocket and became a wooden doll again.

So Vassilissa could spend the day resting. When evening drew on she cooked the supper, laid the table, and sat down to wait for the witch. After a while she heard horse's hooves, and the man in black on a coal-black horse galloped up to the gate and disappeared like a dark shadow. Instantly it became dark, and the eyes of the skulls began glittering.

Then the trees of the forest began to creak and groan, and the bushes and leaves began sighing, and the Baba Yaga came riding out of the dark wood in her mortar, using the pestle as a whip, and sweeping behind her with the broom. Vassilissa let her in, and she went all round the hut, poking into every crevice, looking for faults in the girl's work. But hard as she tried, she could find none. There was not a weed in the yard, nor a speck of dust in the hut, and every black grain had been carefully picked out of the millet.

The witch had to pretend that she was pleased. 'All right,' she said grudgingly, 'you have done well.' Then she clapped her hands and shouted: 'Ho, my servants! Grind my millet!' Immediately three pairs of hands appeared, picked up the sack and took it away.

The Baba Yaga sat down to supper, and Vassilissa brought the food from the oven for her, and *kwas*, mead and wine. The old witch ate it all, crunching the bones – enough for ten men. Then she grew sleepy and said: 'Do the same tomorrow. But this time take the sack of poppy-seed from the store room and go through it, one seed at a time. Someone has mixed earth with the seeds and I want them perfectly clean.' Then she clambered up on the stove and was soon asleep.

As soon as she felt it was safe, Vassilissa took the doll from her pocket, and when she had fed it and seen it come alive she told it what the new task was. 'Never fear,' said the doll. 'I can take care of all that. You go to sleep as you did last night.' So Vassilissa said her prayers, lay down on the floor, and did not wake until she heard the witch whistling in the yard next morning. She got to the window in time to see the old hag climb into her iron mortar, and as she did so the man in red on his red horse leapt over the wall and was gone, and the sun rose over the forest.

It was the same this morning as it had been the day before. All the tasks had been already done, and there was not a speck of earth in among the poppy-seeds. Vassilissa spent an easy day, cooked the supper in the afternoon and put it in the oven, then in the evening laid the table and sat down to wait for the witch. Soon the man in black came galloping up on his coal-black horse, the dark fell, and the eyes in the skulls lit up. Then the forest began to quake and the Baba Yaga swept into sight in her mortar.

She stormed into the house, but although she poked and pried and sniffed into every corner, she could find nothing to fault. And every morsel of dust had disappeared from the poppy-seeds. She clapped her hands and commanded her invisible servants to take away the sack and press the seeds for oil. As before, three pairs of hands appeared and the sack was carried off.

Then the old witch sat down and Vassilissa brought her food and drink enough for twelve men, and she stuffed it all down while the girl stood by silently. 'Well, why are you drooping there like that? Haven't you got a word to say for yourself?'

'I didn't dare speak,' said Vassilissa. 'But I would like to ask some questions, grandmother.'

'Very well,' said the witch. 'But bear in mind that questions very often lead to no good. Remember the proverb, if you know too much you will grow old too soon.'

'I wondered about the men on horseback,' said Vassilissa. 'On the way to your house, a rider all in white passed me.'

'That was my white, bright day,' said the Baba Yaga angrily. 'He is a servant of mine, but he cannot hurt you. What more?'

'Afterwards,' said Vassilissa, 'a rider dressed in red, on a red horse overtook me. Who was he?'

'Another servant,' said the Baba Yaga, grinding her teeth, 'the round red sun. He cannot injure you either. Well, any more?'

'There is a third rider,' said Vassilissa. 'He wears black and rides a black horse, and comes galloping up to your gate every night.'

'That is my servant, the dark night,' said the witch furiously. 'He can do you no harm either. Ask me more.'

But Vassilissa, remembering the Baba Yaga's warning, was silent.

'Ask me more!' the old witch screamed at her. 'Why don't you ask me more? Ask me about the three pairs of hands that serve me!'

But Vassilissa answered prudently, 'You have warned me yourself, grandmother, that people grow old through knowing too much.'

'And if you had asked me about anything in this house,' said the Baba Yaga, 'about those hands, for instance, the hands would have seized you and turned you into food for me. Now, I've got a question of my own. How did you manage to do all the tasks I set for you? Come on, out with it!'

Vassilissa was so terrified at the savage way the witch ground her teeth that she was on the point of telling her about the doll, but she stopped herself just in time and answered: 'The blessing of my dead mother helps me.'

Then the Baba Yaga was in a frenzy of anger. 'Get out of my house this instant!' she screamed. 'No one who bears a blessing can stay in this house! Be off with you!'

Vassilissa ran into the yard, the locks opened, the gates swung wide, and the witch seized one of the skulls with burning eyes and flung it after her. 'There is the fire you wanted,' she howled. 'Your stepmother's daughters sent you in search of it; may they have joy of it!'

So Vassilissa put it at the end of a stick and ran through the forest, finding her way by the light in the eyes which only went out when day had come. At last, by the evening of the next day, when the eyes in the skull were beginning to glimmer again, she came out of the dark forest and saw her stepmother's house. 'Surely they will have found some fire by this time,' she thought, and threw the skull in the hedge. But it spoke to her: 'Do not throw me away, beautiful Vassilissa,' it begged, 'bring me to your stepmother.' And Vassilissa, seeing no light in any of the windows, picked up the skull.

The stepmother and her daughters were, for a wonder, glad to see Vassilissa. The fact was that since she had gone they had had neither fire nor light. They could not cook their food nor warm themselves, and had to sit in darkness. If they tried to strike flint and steel, the tinder would not catch, and the fire they brought from the neighbours would go out as soon as they carried it into the house. But the light in the skull that Vassilissa carried did not go out, to their very great relief, and the stepmother carried it into the best room and set it on a candlestick.

But the eyes of the skull suddenly began to glow like red coals, and wherever the three women turned the eyes followed them, until they were like two furnaces, and grew hotter and hotter until the merchant's wife and her two daughters were burned to ashes. Only Vassilissa was left unharmed.

In the morning she dug a deep hole in the ground and buried the skull. Then she locked the house and went off to the village. Here she found an old woman who was poor and childless, who was willing to take her in until such time as her father came back from the far-distant kingdom.

To while away the time she asked the old woman to provide her with some flax so that she could spin. Her fingers were so deft that the thread came out as even and as fine as a hair, and presently she had enough to weave. But the thread was so fine that there was no frame in the village that it could be woven on, nor indeed any weaver able to do the work.

So once again Vassilissa turned to the doll for help, and the doll said: 'Bring me an old frame and an old basket and some horse hair, and I will contrive something for you.' Vassilissa found all that the doll had asked for, and in the morning, there was a frame, all ready for her to weave her fine thread upon.

All through the winter months Vassilissa sat there weaving, until the whole length of linen was finished, so fine that it could be passed through the eye of a needle. Then when the spring came she bleached it till it was whiter than snow. She told the old woman to take it to market and sell it, and keep the money for herself. But the old woman said: 'This linen is far too good for the market. No one should wear it except the Tsar.'

So next morning the woman carried it to the Tsar's palace and walked up and down in front of it. Servants came out to ask her what she wanted, but she would tell them nothing.

At last the Tsar himself opened a window and asked her what her business was. 'O Tsar's Majesty,' replied the woman, 'I have a piece of linen so miraculously fine that only your eyes should see it.'

The Tsar became curious, and had her brought before him. When he saw the workmanship he was astounded, and asked her what her price was. 'There is no price that can buy it,' she answered. 'I have brought it as a gift.'

The Tsar was much moved, and sent her back home with many rich gifts. Then he called for seamstresses to make the linen into shirts. But no matter how skilled they were, they found that none of them could sew such fine material. At last the Tsar called back the old woman and said: 'If you know enough to weave this linen then you must be able to stitch it too.'

But the old woman said: 'Little Father Tsar, I was not the weaver. It is the work of my adopted daughter.'

'Take it then,' said the Tsar, 'and ask her to sew it for me.'

When the old woman brought it back, Vassilissa locked herself into her own room and began to make the shirts. With the doll's help she could work so fast that soon a dozen were ready. The woman took them to the Tsar, and Vassilissa sat by her window waiting. Presently a servant in royal livery came running. 'The Tsar, our lord, wishes to see the needle-woman who has made his shirts,' he called.

When Vassilissa was led into the Tsar's presence he fell in love with her at once. 'They were right to call you Vassilissa the Beautiful,' he said, 'for there is no one more beautiful than you in all my tsardom. You shall be my wife.'

So the Tsar and Vassilissa were married. The merchant returned from his travels and he and the old woman lived in the palace very happily. And to the end of her life, Vassilissa the Beautiful carried her little doll with her wherever she went.

LITTLE BEAR CUB

ONCE upon a time, far away to the north of this world, there lived an old peasant and his wife, whose great grief was that they had no children. They were honest and hard-working, but very poor, and the old man tried to make a living by hunting wolves and bears and selling their skins.

One day when he had tracked a bear to its den, to his astonishment he found there a little boy of about three years old, naked and sturdy, whom the bear had been rearing like a cub. The peasant carried him home, called in the priest, and had him christened Ivashko Medvedko, which means Little Ivan the Bear Cub.

The child grew up at such a rate that by the time he was fifteen he was man's size and so strong that he could break the other boys' arms just in friendly play. Naturally this did not go down well with the boys' parents, and finally they came to the old peasant and told him that his adopted son would have to go; he was too much of a threat to the other children.

The old man and his wife were very sad for they loved the lad and knew that he meant no harm. 'What are you going to do?' lamented the peasant. 'How are you going to live?'

'Don't fret, little grandfather,' said the boy, 'you'll find I can look after myself. Go and buy me a sturdy iron club – one that weighs a hundredweight ought to be big enough. I'll stay here a week or two and exercise with it, and then I'll go off and seek my fortune.'

The old man managed to find one, loaded it on to his cart and brought it home, and Little Bear Cub began to train himself with it. Now nearby was a field where there were three fir trees; the first was fifteen feet around, the second twenty, and the third twenty-five. At the end of the first week the boy managed to seize the top of the first tree and pull it over. At the end of the second week's exercising he bent the second tree down to the ground and broke it into two pieces. And at the end of the third week he was strong enough to pull up the third tree by the roots. 'Now,' said Little Bear Cub, 'I'm strong enough to take on anything, even a witch.' And so he said goodbye to his foster parents, tucked the club into his belt and went off.

After a while he came to a broad river. On its bank knelt a giant, tall as a birch sapling and broad as a barrel, with his mouth stretched wide in the water, catching fish with his moustache. When he caught one he kindled a fire on his tongue, roasted the fish and swallowed it.

'Good health to you, giant,' said Little Bear Cub. 'Who are you?'

'Your good health,' said the giant. 'My name is Usynia – Whiskers to you. Where are you going?'

'Wherever my eyes look,' said Little Bear Cub. 'Why don't you come too? Two's company, they say, and you look strong enough to be useful.'

'As to that,' said the giant, 'I'm nothing beside the man they call Ivashko Medvedko. Now there really is a strong man.'

'Ivashko Medvedko? – that's me,' said Bear Cub.

'Then I'll come along with you sure enough,' said the giant.

So they travelled on together, and presently they came to a valley where another giant was at work. This one was twelve feet high and he was carrying earth, a whole hill at a time, and mending the roads with it.

'Good health!' called Little Bear Cub. 'What is your name?'

'Good health,' said the giant. 'They call me Gorynia, that is to say Hill-man. Where are you off to?'

'We're following our eyes,' said Bear Cub. 'You're a strong man, I see, and you're working very hard.'

'There are no wars and so there's nothing to do,' said the giant. 'But for strength now, they say there's nothing to beat Ivashko Medvedko.'

'And here he stands before you,' said Bear Cub.

'Then take me with you and I'll be your younger brother,' said the giant. And he left his road-making and journeyed on with the other two.

After two days they reached a forest of oaks, and in it they saw a giant as tall as a barn hard at work levelling all the trees.

'You are indeed a man of might,' said Little Bear Cub. 'What are you called?'

'I go by the name of Dubynia – Oak-man,' said the giant.
'But if it's might you're talking about, then they all say that
Ivashko Medvedko's your man.'

'Which is me,' said Bear Cub. 'Why not join us?'

'Why not?' said the giant.

So now there were four of them tramping through the
world. But after three days Bear Cub had had enough.
'There's no point in pressing further. Why don't we stop
here? There's game in plenty to feed us, and timber enough
to build a house. We could live in style and comfort.'

The giants agreed, and they all set to to clear the ground
and to uproot and trim the trees. By nightfall the roof was on
and the house was ready – big enough to hold forty men
comfortably. The next morning they went off hunting, and
killed enough game to fill the larder. There was venison and
bear meat and wild boar, to say nothing of duck and goose
and ptarmigan and other sorts of fowl. 'Right,' said Bear
Cub, 'that will see us through one day. But we must work to
keep up the stocks. Three of us will have to hunt every day,
and the fourth one must stay at home to guard the house and
to cook. We'd better cast lots to see who shall stay at home
tomorrow.'

It fell to Usynia to be the first to stay behind, and the next
morning while the others went off he hacked up the carcasses
in the larder, plucked and dressed the fowls, then he boiled
and baked and roasted to make a good evening meal. When
everything was in order he sat down by the window to wait
for his comrades' return.

Suddenly the sky darkened, the wind moaned in the trees and the ground began to shake. As he looked out he saw the earth parting. A huge stone a short distance from the house rolled away, and out came a Baba Yaga, riding in a great iron mortar, driving it with the pestle, and sweeping away her trail with a kitchen broom. What was more she was making for the house. Usynia was frightened, but knowing that you have to humour witches he opened the door, wished her good health and invited her in.

'Give me something to eat,' snarled the Baba Yaga. 'Haven't you any manners?''

Usynia took a roast duck from the oven and put it in front of her, with some bread and salt. She crammed it all into her mouth and then looked around for more. He brought her a haunch of venison but it was too small for her liking. 'Is this the way you use a guest?' she shrieked, and she seized him by his moustache, dragged him from side to side of the room, beat him with her iron pestle, and flung him down. Then she cut a strip of skin from his back, snatched all the meat that was in the oven, gobbled it down bones and all, and drove away in her mortar.

When the other three came back they found Usynia sitting on the floor groaning with a handkerchief tied round his head. 'Little brothers,' he said, 'there is no supper. The oven is new and smokes so badly that it gave me a headache.'

The next day it was Gorynia's turn to stay at home. He was determined to do better than Usynia, and when he had filled the oven with good things he sat down, pleased with himself, to wait for the others to come home. Then he heard the wind rising and hail beating on the roof. He looked out of the window and saw the ground heaving and the rock moving. As he watched a Baba Yaga came out in an iron mortar and rode up to the door. Though he was trembling with fear, Gorynia opened the door and asked her in.

'Food!' she shouted at him. 'Can't you see I'm ravenous?'

He put a roast goose and a cup of *kwas* on the table in front of her, but it had disappeared down her throat before you could say knife, and she was yelling for more. This time he brought her bear-steaks, and she was insulted. 'You call this a proper-sized helping! A gnat would be hungry after it!' And she grabbed him with her bony fingers, beat his head against the wall, and pounded at him with her iron pestle. Then she cut a strip from his back, threw him under the table, and ate everything that was in the oven.

As dusk fell the hunters returned. But no smell of roasting meat greeted them as they came into the house. Instead they found Gorynia sitting with his head bandaged. 'It's no good, little brothers,' he told them, 'you'll have to do without a proper supper today. The wood was damp and my head's aching fit to split from trying to blow at the flames.' So the hunters went to bed hungry for a second night.

Next day Dubynia stayed at home, and the same thing happened. The Baba Yaga came out of the ground from underneath the rock, stormed into the house, ate all the supper, cut a strip of flesh from his back, then beat him to a jelly with her pestle. 'I'm sorry, little brothers,' he said to his companions when they came in and found him with his head in his hands, 'the oven has been playing me up. The wood burnt all right, but the dampers don't work and the fumes have been pouring into the kitchen and given me a right old headache.' So again the hunters missed their meal.

On the fourth day it was Bear Cub's turn to be house-keeper. He tidied everything, then fried and stewed and roasted and baked till the house was full of delicious smells. Then he washed himself and sat down by the window. Suddenly he noticed that there was lashing rain, and the trees of the forest were rocking and swaying. Then the earth parted in front of the house, the rock rolled away, and out rode the Baba Yaga in her iron mortar.

But Bear Cub was not in the least frightened. He put his hundredweight iron club handy by the door and went out to greet his guest. 'Health to you, grandmother!' he called. She pushed past him and hobbled into the house. 'Food!' she shouted, 'and make it quick!'

'There's nothing here for you,' said Bear Cub.

Grinding her iron teeth the Baba Yaga sprang at him, but he was too fast for her, and snatched up his iron club and beat her until she howled for mercy. Then he threw her into a cupboard and locked the door.

Presently the three giants returned. Each one, though he said nothing to the others, expected to find Bear Cub beaten up and all the supper gone. But he opened the door, wel-comed them, and brought all sorts of delicious food from the oven. As they fell on it they eyed him furtively and decided that he had been spared a visit from the Baba Yaga.

When at last supper was over and they sat belching with satisfaction and picking their teeth, Bear Cub went to heat the bath. Now the giants felt very ashamed of the strips that the witch had cut from their backs, and they all tried to stand so that they faced Bear Cub. 'What's wrong with you that you keep on spinning round?' he said at last. 'You make me giddy.' Then he saw the scars on their shoulders.

Usynia said: 'The day I stayed at home I fell against the oven door and got burnt.' Gorynia said: 'An ember shot out when I turned my back.' And Dubynia said: 'The fumes from the burning wood made me so dizzy that I fell and did myself an injury.'

Bear Cub roared with laughter, opened the cupboard door and dragged out the Baba Yaga by the hair. 'Here you are,' he said, 'here's your oven door, your ember and your fumes.'

Now the old witch was cunning and at first she played possum, lying on the floor with her eyes closed, pretending to be dead. When they were all off their guard she jumped up, seized her mortar and disappeared into the ground outside, beneath the great rock. The giants were too late to stop her. They all rushed to the rock but they couldn't shift it. Then Bear Cub strolled over, lifted the rock and hurled it far away among the trees. Beneath it was an enormous dark hole.

'She's down here somewhere,' he said, 'and she's out to get us. If we don't kill her she'll kill us. So who's game to go after her?'

The giants looked at each other sheepishly. Usynia hid

behind Gorynia, and Gorynia slunk behind Dubynia, and
Dubynia stared up at the sky as though he had not heard.

'Oh well,' said Bear Cub, 'it'll have to be me. But you must
help me make a rope to get down there.'

So they all set to cutting up the hides of the animals they
had killed, and they knotted the strips and twisted them
until they had a good long rope. Bear Cub planted a post in
the ground, tied one end of the rope to it, and threw the other
end into the hole. 'Now, little brothers,' he said. 'You stay
here and watch. If you see the rope shake then pull it up
straight away and haul me out.' Then he filled his pouch with
food, and lowered himself down the hole.

The rope held, and it was long enough. At the bottom of
the hole there was a path, and when he had stumbled along
this for a while he found himself in a new world. It looked
very like the upper world he had come from – there were
trees and grass and sky – but there was no sign of human life,
indeed no life at all except for flocks of huge birds flying high
overhead. He wandered on, desolate and lonely, and after
four days he came to a little hut among the trees. It was
perched on chicken legs and was whirling round and round,
and there outside was a beautiful girl. Overjoyed to see life at
last he ran towards her.

She looked at him with amazement. 'Where have you
come from? Don't you know the danger you are in? This is a
Baba Yaga's house; she's asleep at the moment but if she
smells you she'll eat you.'

'I'm a match for any Baba Yaga,' boasted Bear Cub. 'You

should have seen what I did to one in the upper world the other day.'

'You're a brave man,' said the girl. 'But you'll find it's different here – she's a hundred times more powerful now she's back home. I tell you what, though – hide in the trees until she rides out in her mortar, and I may be able to help you get the better of her. Only you must promise that if you do you will take me back with you to the upper world where I belong.'

'That's for sure,' said Bear Cub, looking at her admiringly. So he went and climbed a tree and hid himself among its leaves. Presently he felt the ground heave and the trees shake, and the Baba Yaga came riding out of the hut in her mortar, driving it along with the pestle, and sweeping the trail behind her with a broom. He came down from his hiding place and the girl came out of the hut to meet him. She showed him two huge casks of water.

'Do as I say,' she commanded. 'Drink from the cask on the right.'

So he cupped his hands, scooped up some and drank. 'More,' she told him. And he went on drinking. 'Now,' she said, 'how strong do you feel?'

'Strong enough to send this hut spinning away over the forest,' he told her.

'Better take some more,' she said.

So he went on drinking. 'How do you feel now?' she asked.

'Strong enough to hold the whole forest in one hand,' he said.

'Listen, then,' she said. 'The water in your cask is the Water of Strength, and it's this that makes the Baba Yaga so powerful. The other cask has Weak Water in it, and whoever drinks from that becomes as weak as the water itself. What you have got to do is change them over. Then when the Baba Yaga comes in, grab her pestle and whatever you do, don't let go. She'll try to get it from you but she won't be able to. So she'll make for the Water of Strength which she thinks is in the right-hand cask. But what she will drink will be Weak Water. That's your moment – you can kill her then. But mind you use only one stroke. Her mortar, her pestle and her broom will tell you to strike again, but if you do she will come to life.'

Bear Cub changed the position of the casks as the girl had told him, and then went outside to wait for the Baba Yaga. When he felt the ground shaking and heard the trees sighing he knew that she was near. Up she rode in her mortar and went into the house. She began snuffing the air. 'There's a Russian smell here and no mistake,' she screeched. 'Who's been in this house?'

'No one has been here, grandmother,' said the girl. 'How could anyone from the upper world find his way to this place?'

'True enough,' said the Baba Yaga. 'The only one I'm afraid of is Ivashko Medvedko and he's so far off that a crow would take a year to fly here with one of his bones.'

'You're wrong there!' shouted Bear Cub, and he sprang out from behind the bush where he had been hiding and seized her iron pestle. The Baba Yaga howled and spat, but she couldn't shake him off. She dragged him here and she dragged him there, trying to dash him to pieces against the stones, to drown him in the river, and threatening him with horrible torture. But Bear Cub had drunk Water of Strength and she could do nothing with him. So finally she flung down the pestle and went over to the casks and began to drink from the one on the right side. Instantly all the strength flowed out of her, and Bear Cub, drawing his sword, cut off her head.

'Strike again! Strike again!' the iron mortar, the pestle and the broom called.

'A brave man does not strike twice,' he said, sheathing his sword. Then he made a fire and burnt her wicked body to ashes and set out with the girl for the upper world.

On the second day of their journey there was a fierce storm of rain, and they sheltered under a tree. Bear Cub noticed a nest in a bush, belonging to one of the huge birds he had seen flying overhead. It was full of fledglings, and pitying the young ones in this downpour he put his cloak over the bush to protect them. Then when the rain stopped he took the girl by the hand and they walked on till they reached the underground passage. There they made their way through the dark till they reached the bottom of the hole where the hide-rope was hanging. Bear Cub tied the girl to it and shook it. The giant up above whose turn it was to keep watch ran to fetch the other two, and between them they pulled her up.

But Bear Cub's troubles were not over yet, for when the

giants saw how beautiful the girl was, each one desired her
for himself. Though they could not decide which one of them
should have her, they were all agreed that it should not be
Bear Cub. So when it was his turn and they had hauled him
nearly to the top of the hole, they cut the rope and let him fall
right down to the bottom.

Bruised and shaken he lay there for two days and then he
picked himself up and wandered back down the passage into
the world he had just left. As he wandered aimlessly, not
knowing what to do, a bird almost his own size came flying
up. 'Ivashko Medvedko,' it said to him in Russian, 'you had
pity on my fledglings, and for this I owe you a service. What
can I do for you?'

'All that I want,' said Bear Cub, 'is to find my way back to
the upper world.'

'That's not as easy as you might think,' said the bird. 'But
we'll try. The journey will take a long time though, and we'll
need provisions. Twist yourself a basket out of osier twigs,
then go into the forest and fill it with mushrooms and berries
and nuts. When you are ready get on to my back with the
basket and we'll set off. I won't ever stop, but when I turn
my head you'll know I'm hungry and then you must feed
me.'

Bear Cub did what he was told, and when all the preparations were complete the bird flew off. Whether it was a
long time or a short time no one can tell now, but at last when
the provisions were nearly all gone, the bird flew out into the
upper world and set him down in a green meadow. And after

that he still had to find his way back to his own part of the world.

But he got there, and as he trudged the last stretch towards the house he and the giants had built he could see, sitting on the step, the girl whom he had brought back from the underworld. She gave a cry of joy and ran towards him. The giants had been quarrelling night and day over her, she said. But they still couldn't decide which one should have her, and in the meantime she was forced to be their servant.

'None of them shall have you,' he said, kissing her. 'You shall be *my* bride.'

He went up to the house, and there he could see through the window the three giants sitting and drinking. He pulled his cap down over his face and in a humble voice asked for a cup of *kwas*.

'Be off with you!' grunted Usynia. 'We don't have anything for beggars.'

'Do you want a taste of my club?' snarled Gorynia.

'I'll set the dogs on you!' shouted Dubynia.

Then Bear Cub took off his cap. They recognized him at once and turned pale with fright. They made for the door and ran off as if a Tartar army was behind them, and were never seen again. So Bear Cub married the beautiful girl he had rescued, and they lived in that house in peace and comfort for a long, long time.

MARYA MOREVNA

ALONG way away, and a long time ago, there was a Tsar who had one son, Tsarevich Alexis, and three daughters, the Tsarevnas Anna, Olga and Elena. When he grew old and lay dying he called his son to him. 'I put your sisters in your charge,' he said. 'Care for them lovingly, but do not delay their marriage. Whoever asks the hand of any one of them, let him wed her – provided that she gives her consent.'

After the Tsar's death the three sisters often used to recall their father's words and wonder what sort of suitors would come for them, and which would be the first to marry. One day they were walking in the garden with their brother when the sun was suddenly overcast with a huge black cloud in the shape of a hawk. 'Let us hurry indoors, little sisters,' said the Tsarevich Alexis. 'There is going to be a fearful storm.' They ran inside, and just as they reached the palace there was a crash of thunder, the roof opened and a hawk came flying in. As it struck the ground it changed into a handsome youth.

'Greetings, Tsarevich Alexis,' said the youth. 'I come as a suitor to ask for the hand of your sister Anna.'

'If she agrees then so shall I,' said the Tsarevich. The youth was so winning that the Tsarevna put her hand in his at once. They were married that day and set out for the Hawk's tsardom.

After that the days ran swiftly until a year had passed and it was summer once more. The Tsarevich was walking again with his two sisters in the garden when they saw the sky darkening. There was a cloud like a huge black eagle with lightning flashing across it. 'Run, little sisters,' called their brother, 'before the storm breaks.' Thunder broke above their heads as they ran into the palace, and through the ceiling came an eagle. It alighted on the floor and turned into a tall young man with a radiant face.

'Good health, Tsarevich Alexis,' said he. 'I have come to this kingdom to ask you to give me your sister Olga as a wife.'

'Is this what you wish, little sister?' the Tsarevich asked.

The Eagle was even more handsome than the Hawk, and the Tsarevna readily agreed. So they were married and she went back with him to his own country.

Another year went by, and once again the Tsarevich was in the garden, this time only with his youngest sister. As they strolled among the flowers they saw a fierce black cloud shaped like a crow blot out the sun. 'Run quickly, little sister,' called the Tsarevich, 'a hurricane is approaching.'

But it was no hurricane that split the palace roof. Instead a black crow came through the ceiling, settled on the ground and turned into a young man of even more dazzling good looks than the Hawk or the Eagle. 'I wish you prosperity, Tsarevich Alexis,' he said. 'I have come to your palace to ask if you will allow your sister Elena to be my wife.'

'If she is willing then let it be,' said the brother. And so the last sister departed.

The Tsarevich grew sad alone in the palace, and when a year went by without sight or sound of his sisters, he decided to go in search of them. So he ordered his horse to be saddled and went off. He rode on and on, and after much journeying he came to a vast plain where a huge army lay dead and dying, their weapons scattered all round them. He sat there on his horse, staring around him at this terrible sight, and called out: 'If there is anyone left alive, let him tell me what has happened.' And a soldier, the last living of the whole host, raised his head. 'We have all been destroyed by Marya Morevna, the warrior princess.' And he fell back to the ground and died.

Brooding on all this, the Tsarevich rode on, and not long afterwards saw white tents pitched in the distance. As he drew nearer a beautiful young woman came out of one of them. This was Marya Morevna herself. 'Greeting, Tsarevich Alexis,' she said. 'Have you come of your own free will?'

И. БИЛИБИНЪ. 1901

'Tsarevna, brave men do not do anything against their will,' said the Tsarevich proudly.

She was pleased with this answer. 'Stay with me here as my guest,' she told him. So he dismounted, and went with her. Before two days had passed they had fallen in love, and he went back with her to her palace where they were married.

They lived in happiness for several months, but then news came of a rebellion in a distant part of Marya Morevna's kingdom, and she was obliged to set off with her army to crush it. 'Look after the palace while I am away,' she told her husband. 'Only whatever you do, don't open the door of the locked closet in my inner chamber.'

The Tsarevich promised to obey, but she had not long been gone before curiosity overcame him and he unlocked the closet door. And there to his astonishment he saw an old, old man, writhing on the wall to which he was chained with twelve chains.

'Who are you?' asked the Tsarevich.

'I am the wizard Kashchey the Deathless,' gasped the old man. 'Marya Morevna's father imprisoned me here, and I have suffered tortures for ten years. You have a kind face; bring just a drop of water to ease my torment.'

The Tsarevich pitied the sufferings of the poor creature, filled a cup and brought it to him. The wizard swallowed it at a single gulp. 'After all these years my thirst is great,' he said. 'I pray you bring me more, and I will give you your life when danger threatens.'

This time the Tsarevich came back with a jugful. The

wizard tossed it back and pleaded again. 'Just one last drink,' he begged, 'and twice I will give you your life when otherwise you would perish.'

The Tsarevich brought water in a bucket, and Kashchey emptied it without drawing breath. This time all his strength returned; he strained at the twelve chains and they snapped like rotten thread. 'My thanks, Tsarevich,' he shouted. 'You are now as likely to have your Marya Morevna again as to see your own ears!' He flew out of the window in a whirlwind, overtook Marya Morevna at the head of her army and carried her away across three times nine tsardoms to his own land.

Tsarevich Alexis wept bitterly when he saw what his disobedience had brought about. Then he told himself that come what might, he would never rest until he found his princess again, and he set out on his quest.

He rode one day, he rode two days, and at dawn on the third day he came to a beautiful palace whose roof shone like a rainbow. An oak tree stood near, and on its topmost branch a hawk perched. As soon as it saw him, it flew down and turned into a handsome youth. 'Welcome, my dear brother-in-law,' he cried. 'How has God dealt with you these past three years?' And Tsarevna Anna came running out to embrace her brother.

They pressed him to stay there with them, but after three days he said: 'It is time now to depart. I must go on with my search for my wife, Marya Morevna.'

'A long journey lies ahead of you,' his brother-in-law said

sadly. 'Leave your silver spoon with us. When we look at it then we shall be reminded of you.'

The Tsarevich left the spoon and rode on. He rode one day, he rode a second, and on the third he came to a palace even finer than the one he had left, with a roof of mother-of-pearl. In front stood a fir tree, and an eagle flew down from it as the Tsarevich drew near. The eagle became a young man when it touched the ground. 'Come quickly, wife,' he called. 'Here is our brother Alexis!' And Tsarevna Olga hastened out, and both she and her husband questioned the Tsarevich and pressed hospitality on him.

When three days had gone by the Tsarevich made his farewell. He could tarry no longer, he said, but must resume his search for Marya Morevna.

'It is many versts* to the castle of Kashchey,' said the Eagle. 'Leave us a souvenir of your coming. Leave us your silver fork.'

He gave them the fork, mounted, and went on his way. On the third day of his journey he found himself approaching a palace of porphyry, larger than the Hawk's or the Eagle's put together, and roofed with golden tiles. A crow flew down from a birch tree as he rode up, and was transformed into a graceful youth. 'Tsarevna Elena!' he called, 'come and greet your brother!' And the Tsarevich embraced the sister that he had not seen for over a year. But, as before, he grew restless after three days and told his hosts that he must continue his search for his wife.

*a verst is about $\frac{2}{3}$ mile

'Your search may be in vain,' the Crow warned him, 'for Kashchey the Deathless is both powerful and cunning. Leave your silver snuff-box with us so that we can look at it and think of you.'

Leaving the snuff-box with them, the Tsarevich again set out. And after many weary weeks at last he came to Kashchey's castle. He knew it at once, for there in the garden he could see his dear Marya Morevna. She threw herself upon him and sobbed. 'O Tsarevich Alexis! Why did you disobey me? See what you have done!'

'I am guilty before you,' said the Tsarevich sadly. 'But escape with me now while he is out of sight. Perhaps he may not be able to overtake us.'

Now that day Kashchey had gone hunting. As he rode back to the castle in the evening his horse stumbled. 'What are you about, you miserable bag of bones?' he shrieked at it. 'If there is something wrong, tell me.'

'There is certainly something wrong,' said the horse. 'Tsarevich Alexis has carried off your Marya Morevna.'

'Can you catch them up?' demanded the wizard.

'If you were to sow a sack of wheat, wait for it to grow,' said the horse, tossing its head, 'harvest it and thresh it, grind the grain to flour and then bake five ovens of bread to eat, after that I should still be able to catch them up.'

Kashchey whipped the horse to a gallop and easily overtook the Tsarevich. He snatched up Marya Morevna. 'I ought to kill you for this,' he said to her husband. 'Still, I

promised you your life when you brought me water, so I'll spare you this time.'

The Tsarevich wept, but weeping never did anyone any good, and he decided to wait till morning and then go back to the castle again. 'Fly with me!' he urged the princess when he found her in the garden. 'At least we shall have a few hours together.' And he put her on his horse and they rode off.

Kashchey had gone out hunting that day too, and when he rode back in the evening his horse stumbled as he had done the previous day. 'Now what's wrong?' shouted the wizard. 'Are you telling me you've cast a shoe? Or is it something more important?'

'More important to you than to me,' said the horse. 'That young whippersnapper has stolen Marya Morevna again.'

'Can we overtake them?' said the wizard.

'Master,' said the horse, 'you could scatter barley, wait till harvest time, cut it, thresh it, brew beer from the grain, and drink the beer till you were tipsy. Even if you waited till you were sober, I could still catch those two.'

And so Kashchey caught them up before they had gone very far. 'You fool!' he bawled at the Tsarevich. 'Didn't I tell you that you could as easily see your own ears as take back Marya Morevna? Well, I made you a promise so I suppose I'm obliged to give you your life this second time. But after this, beware!'

The Tsarevich wept as he saw his dear wife snatched up again, but he was not daunted, and the next morning he went back to the castle yet again. Marya Morevna tried to resist

him. 'The Wizard will not spare you this time,' she warned
him. But he answered: 'If I cannot live with you, then I will
not live without you!' And he lifted her on to his saddle
before him and rode off.

As Kashchey came back after his day's hunting, his horse
began to stumble from side to side. 'A fresh calamity, is it?'
grumbled the wizard. 'Well, tell me the worst!'

'It's that young prince, of course,' the horse told him.
'He's been here yet again after Marya Morevna.'

'And can we outstrip them?' said the wizard.

'You could sow flax-seed,' said the horse, 'wait till it's ripe,
then pick it, clean it and card it. You could spin the thread,
weave the cloth, sew a shirt, wear that shirt to shreds. Even
with all that to do first, I could outstrip them.'

'You set about it then!' the wizard yelled. And he had
hardly uttered the words before the horse was there. He
snatched Marya Morevna from the saddle and put her on his
own horse. 'As for you,' he said grimly to the Tsarevich, 'I
was obliged to spare your life twice, but this time I'm free to
do as I choose, and I choose to rid myself of you for ever.'
And he drew out his sword and hacked the young man to
pieces. He took the pieces back to the castle, had them put
into a barrel hooped with iron, and ordered servants to throw
the barrel into the sea.

Now the Hawk, the Eagle and the Crow and their wives
often used to look at the silver spoon, the fork and the snuff-
box and wonder how their brother was faring. One day they
suddenly saw that the three pieces of silver were turning

black, and they knew that the Tsarevich was in great danger. The Hawk flew to the Eagle, and the Eagle and he set out for the Crow. Then having discussed a plan of action, the Crow flew west, the Eagle to the east, and the Hawk to the north. They searched all day, and in the evening met again to confer.

'I saw nothing,' said the Hawk, 'except a band of crows heading south.'

'I met them,' said the Crow, 'and they reported having sighted something afloat in the sea.'

'Brothers,' said the Hawk, 'we must go and see what that something is.'

They flew to where the cask was floating, pulled it to shore, and found inside it the limbs, the head and the trunk of the dead Tsarevich. The Hawk flew to find the water of life, and the Crow went for the water of death. When the water of death was sprinkled on the pieces they grew together again, and when the Hawk poured his water of life over the body the Tsarevich sat up and rubbed his eyes. 'I seem to have overslept,' he said.

'You would have slept even longer if it hadn't been for us,' said his brothers-in-law. 'Now, do come home with one of us.'

But the Tsarevich shook his head; he had to continue his search for Marya Morevna. The three brothers, seeing it was useless to argue, consulted together. Then the Crow said: 'An ordinary horse will always be overtaken by the one Kashchey rides; your only chance is to find something faster. Our advice is to try to discover where it was foaled.'

So once again Tsarevich Alexis rode back to Kashchey's castle to find Marya Morevna. She was in the garden as she had been before. They embraced each other with tears of joy, and he told her why he had come. That night Marya Morevna said to the wizard: 'Tell me, for I have often wondered, about that horse of yours. It's no ordinary animal – look how it overtook the Tsarevich Alexis even when he had a long start! Where was it foaled?'

Kashchey said: 'There is a meadow far away by the sea where a wonderful mare grazes, strong enough to make the sea rise in huge waves when she goes into it, and to fell oak trees when she brushes past them. Every month she bears a foal, but twelve fierce wolves follow her to devour them. Every third year she bears a foal with a white star on its forehead, and whoever beats off the wolves and snatches this one will have a steed like mine.'

'And is this how you got yours, you brave man?' asked Marya Morevna.

'No, not I,' said the wizard. 'A Baba Yaga did it. She lives across three times nine lands, in the thirtieth tsardom, across the River of Fire. It's she who follows the mare and seizes every foal that has a white star. She's got quite a stableful of fine horses now. I once spent three days helping look after them, and she gave me a foal in payment. That's the horse I now ride.'

'But how did you cross the River of Fire?' asked Marya Morevna admiringly.

'Easy enough,' the wizard told her. 'There's a handkerchief in my chest. I only have to wave it three times to my right and there is a bridge so high that the flames cannot reach it.'

As soon as Kashchey was asleep, Marya Morevna took the handkerchief from the chest. Next morning when the Tsarevich came to the garden she gave it to him, and off he went on his weary travels again. He walked one day, he walked two days, he walked three days without anything to eat or drink. When he felt he was nearly dying of hunger he came across a nest of fledglings and snatched up one of them. He was about to kill it and eat it when the mother bird spoke: 'Tsarevich, spare my child! One day I may be able to help you.'

So the prince put back the bird and stumbled on. He had not gone far before he came upon a beehive in the forest, and braving the angry bees he put his hand in to take a piece of honeycomb. But he heard the voice of the queen bee: 'Tsarevich, you will be taking the winter food of my subjects. Leave it, and I promise you will not regret it.'

He put back the honey and went on. The forest ended and he found himself standing on the sea-shore, and in the sand he saw a crayfish. When he picked it up it begged for its life. 'Tsarevich, I will be more use to you alive than dead.' So he let that go too, and went on, so tired and so hungry that he could hardly crawl.

With the help of the magic handkerchief he managed to cross the River of Fire, and found himself standing in front of a hut on chicken legs. There were twelve poles standing round the hut, eleven of them had men's heads on them; the twelfth alone had none.

The prince climbed up the chicken legs and went in. There lay the old witch on the stove, snoring. She woke up as he came in. 'I smell Russian blood,' she said. 'And what do you want, young man?'

'I am hungry and in need of work,' he told her.

'Then you may tend my horses,' she said. 'If you look after them well then I will give you one. But if you lose even one of them then your head will be upon that pole you see outside.'

The Tsarevich agreed to the bargain, and the witch gave him food and drink, then sent him to the stables and ordered him to take the horses into the meadow. Once out of the stable the horses whisked their tails and galloped off in different directions before he had time to seize the halter of even one of them. The Tsarevich watched them disappearing into the distance, and then sat down on a stone and wept.

But very soon he had fallen asleep from exhaustion. He did not wake until it was evening; there was a bird pecking at his sleeve. 'Get up, Tsarevich Alexis,' it was saying to him. 'The horses have been in the meadow and they are all now back in the stable. I have done the service I promised you when you spared my fledgling.'

When the Tsarevich reached the stable he heard the Baba Yaga shouting at the horses. 'Why did you come home?' she was saying angrily.

'What else could we do?' they replied. 'We did as you said and scattered. But then flocks of birds came flying, and pecked at our eyes and drove us back.'

'Well then tomorrow just you keep to the forest. You'll be well hidden among the trees,' said the witch.

Next morning the Baba Yaga sent the Tsarevich out again. 'You take care,' she warned him. 'If any one of those horses is missing when you bring them back in the evening your head goes on that pole!'

He went to the stable and opened the door, and instantly the horses were thundering past him – off into the forest. He sat down mournfully on a stone and, wondering what he could do, fell asleep. When he woke there was a bee buzzing near his face. 'You had better go and look to the horses, Tsarevich Alexis. They are all back in the stable now. I said I might be able to help you.'

And sure enough, there were the horses, each in its own

stall, and the old witch was berating them. 'How could we
help it?' they complained. 'As soon as we got in among the
trees, thousands of angry bees swarmed round us and stung
us and chased us back here.'

'Then you'll have to go into the sea tomorrow, and mind
you swim far out,' she told them.

And when the old witch saw Tsarevich Alexis she laughed
and laughed. 'Your head will certainly be on that last pole
tomorrow!'

And he thought the same next morning, as the horses
galloped past him out of the stable and disappeared in a
cloud of dust. He followed them to the shore, and stood there
gazing out to sea. But by this time there was not a sign of
them, and he lay down on the sand in despair. He woke to
find a crayfish nipping his finger. 'Tsarevich Alexis,' it said, 'I
told you I would be of use to you. The horses are all back in
their stable. You go back too. In a corner you will find a
mangy colt that drags its legs. That's the horse for you!
When midnight comes, take it and ride for your life.'

As Tsarevich Alexis approached the stable he could hear
the old witch, beside herself with rage. 'That was our last
chance for his head!' she was screaming, 'and you have to go
and spoil it!'

'How could we stay in the water?' said the horses sullenly.
'There were crayfish all round us, clawing the flesh from our
bones.'

Grumbling and muttering, the old witch sat down on a
stool, waiting for the Tsarevich. But at last she got weary

and shuffled back to her hut. Then he came out of the shadows, groped his way to the colt, saddled it and was off. He crossed the River of Fire by waving the magic handkerchief three times on his right side. Instantly a high stone bridge sprang up and he led the colt across the flames below. Then he waved the handkerchief twice to his left side, and the bridge shrank to a third of its height and became thin and narrow.

The instant the Baba Yaga woke in the morning she knew what had happened and set out in her mortar, driving it on with her iron pestle. She came to the River of Fire and started to cross the bridge, but the flames licked at her, and the mortar toppled over the edge and she plunged down into the burning abyss.

Meanwhile Tsarevich Alexis pastured his colt in the lush green meadows that had fed the witch's other horses, and it grew and grew until after twelve days it was fit for a hero to ride. Then he mounted and galloped off across the nine times three tsardoms to Kashchey's castle. There was Marya Morevna in the garden, and he told her to get up in the saddle in front of him, for he now had a horse as good as the wizard's.

The wizard had been hunting as usual, and as he came back in the evening his horse fell on one knee. 'Get up, you idle laggard!' screamed the wizard, beating it. 'What's wrong with you? Do you scent danger?'

'I scent disaster,' said the horse. 'The Tsarevich has snatched up Marya Morevna. And this time I doubt whether I can catch up – he is riding my youngest brother.'

But the horse stretched out his neck and galloped like the wind, and he did overtake the Tsarevich. Just as Kashchey raised his sword to kill him, the horse the Tsarevich was riding called out: 'O brother, brother! How can you be a slave to such an unclean monster! Throw him off!'

Kashchey's horse heard his brother and threw Kashchey to the ground and lashed at him with his hooves. And the Tsarevich and his bride rode off, leaving him dead. They called at the palaces of the Hawk, the Eagle and the Crow on their way home, and were received with rejoicing. Then Tsarevich Alexis took Marya Morevna back to his own country, where they lived happily in peace for many years.

FROST

THERE once was an old man who had three daughters. His first wife was dead, and his second wife had no love for the eldest daughter, who was not hers. She was for ever scolding her, and made her the household drudge. The girl had to get up before daybreak, feed and water the cattle, bring in wood for the stove, light the fire, fetch water, clean the room, mend the clothes. Even then the stepmother was never satisfied but would grumble away at Marfa saying: 'What a lazybones! What a slut! Look, she's left this brush in the wrong place and has forgotten to shake out the duster!'

The girl never complained, though she often wept in secret, and tried harder than ever to please her stepmother and her half-sisters. But they, copying their mother, were always insulting Marfa and delighted in making her cry. They were as idle as the day is long. They lay in bed late, letting Marfa fetch and carry for them, and did not sit down to work until after dinner.

The old man felt sorry for his eldest daughter, who was not only industrious and always did what she was bid, but was kind and affectionate too. But he did not know how to help her. He was feeble, his wife was a scold, and his other daughters were as obstinate and cross-grained as they were lazy.

So things went on until all three girls were grown-up and of an age to marry. The old folks started working out how they could get the girls settled in life. The wife, of course, just wanted to rid herself of her stepdaughter as soon as she could, for she knew that no one would make an offer for her own daughters while the pretty, hard-working Marfa was around. So one day she said to her husband: 'I say, old man, it's time Marfa was married. I've got a fine bridegroom in mind for her. You get up early tomorrow morning and harness the mare to the sledge – I'll tell you where to go. And you, Marfa, put your things together in a basket and put on a clean petticoat; you're going off on a visit.'

Marfa was delighted to hear of this treat in store and she slept well all night. She was up long before daybreak, washed herself, said her prayers, then packed her few belongings into a basket. It was midwinter, and bitterly cold outside, with a wind that nearly took off your ears and the ground frozen hard as iron. The old man went outside and harnessed the mare to the sledge. 'Sit down and eat before you go,' called his wife. So he came in and she set some hot tea and bread in front of him. But Marfa only got a saucer of cold cabbage soup left over from the day before.

'Now,' said her stepmother, 'be off, both of you. Drive Marfa to her bridegroom, old greybeard. You've got to turn off the road into the forest, go right up to the big pine that stands on the hill, and there hand her over to Frost.'

The old man stopped eating and stared at his wife in horror. Poor Marfa started crying.

'Now then, what's all this noise about?' demanded the stepmother. 'Your bridegroom is a fine-looking man, and he's so rich! Look at all the things he owns – the fir woods and the pines and the birch trees which he covers with white crystals. Anybody might envy him; he's a hero all right!'

The old man had learnt long ago that it was useless to argue with his wife, so he led his daughter to the sledge, tucked an old blanket round her and set off on the journey. They left the road, and went into the forest and drove among the dark trees. When they had reached the pine tree on the hill he made his daughter get out, and put her basket beside her. Then he turned the horse round and went sadly home.

Marfa sat and shivered. Her clothes were far too thin for the fierce cold. She had not the strength to run away and besides, where could she run to? Her teeth chattered, but her face was too frozen even to cry. Suddenly she heard a sound. Not far away Frost was cracking away on a fir. He was leaping from tree to tree, coming nearer and nearer, and snapping his fingers as he came. Then, there he was, high in the tree above her. 'Are you warm, maiden?' he called.

The air was so cold that it hurt Marfa to breathe, but she said: 'I am warm, Father Frost.'

Frost began to climb down lower, snapping his fingers and cracking the branches as he did. 'Are you still warm, little maid, are you sure?'

Marfa was numb in every limb but she still replied: 'I am quite warm, thank you, dear Father Frost.'

Frost cracked the branches louder than ever. 'Are you

warm, my pretty one? Are you warm now, my darling?'

Marfa just had the strength to whisper: 'Warm, dear Frost, quite warm.' Then Frost felt sorry for her. He jumped down to the ground, wrapped the girl up in rich furs, covered her with warm blankets and filled up her basket with splendid presents.

Next morning the old woman said to her husband. 'Go on, greybeard, you'd better go out and wake the young couple in the forest.' Weeping, the old man set out, dreading what he would find. But there under the pine tree was his daughter alive and well, and singing to herself. She was wearing a wonderful fur cloak and a rich bridal veil; there were costly blankets wrapped round her, and beside her was a basket full of fine linen. Marvelling, the old man loaded it all on the sledge, and drove off home with Marfa.

Her stepmother was thunderstruck when she saw the girl still alive, and the rich gifts that she brought back with her. 'You won't get round me like that!' she shouted. Then she thought over what she should do. That night she told the old man that he had better take the other two girls to the same bridegroom. 'The presents he gave Marfa are nothing to what he'll give them!' she said.

So early next morning she gave her daughters their breakfast, saw to it that they were dressed in their best clothes, and sent them off on their journey. And as before the old man set them down under the tall pine on the hill. There the girls sat laughing and talking.

'Whatever is mother thinking of to send us here!' said one.

'Both of us together, too. As if there weren't enough lads in the village. Heaven knows the sort of rubbishy man who will turn up at a back-of-beyond place like this.'

The girls were wrapped in fur coats, but even so they began to feel the cold. 'I say, Prascovia,' said the other, 'the frost is skinning me alive. If the bridegroom doesn't turn up soon he'll find us laid out stiff.'

'Well, you've just got to put up with it,' snapped her sister. 'As if suitors came in the morning! It's nothing like dinner-time yet.'

'I've just thought, Prascovia. If only one of them comes, which of us will he take?'

'Not you, you stupid goose.'

'You mean it will be you?'

'Indeed that's what I mean.'

'And why you, pray? You seem to think a lot of yourself! Not everybody else does, you know.'

Meanwhile Frost had numbed the girls' hands, so they folded them under their dresses, and went on quarrelling.

'You stupid pig – as if anybody would look at such a fright as you. And lazy too; oh I could tell some tales if I chose!'

'Nothing to what I could tell about you. What use would you be to any husband? You don't know so much as how to begin weaving. And as for your cooking – why, the dogs would turn their backs on it!'

'And you wouldn't even be there to cook or to weave! You'd be gadding around and gossiping the livelong day.'

While the girls went on scolding they began to freeze

and turn blue with cold. 'You do look a fright,' said one, 'all blue and pinched.' Then she listened, for a good way off, Frost had begun snapping his fingers and leaping from tree to tree.

'There he is, Prascovia! He's coming at last, and with bells too.'

'You'd say anything but your prayers! Bells indeed! I can tell you the frost is taking the skin off my fingers.'

But all the time Frost was coming nearer and nearer, cracking the branches, jumping over the trees. At last he reached the pine under which the girls were sitting, and he called: 'Are you warm, young women? Warm enough, eh?'

'Oh Frost, we're nearly perished with cold! We're waiting for a bridegroom but the stupid oaf won't come.'

Frost slid lower down towards them, cracking the branches as he came.

'Are you nice and warm, my darlings? Nice and warm, my pretty ones?'

'Oh give over, do; stop asking such stupid questions! Can't you see our hands and feet are dead with cold?'

Frost came even lower, and his breath was cold on their faces. 'Are you warmer now, my pigeons?'

'Oh shut up and go to hell!' screamed the girls, and next instant fell back, frozen dead.

Next morning the old woman woke her husband early. 'You'd better go and fetch those girls quickly,' she screeched at him. 'There's been a cruel frost all night. Put hay at the bottom of the sledge and take these sheepskin wraps to cover them. Be off with you and don't keep them waiting.' And she bundled him out of the house without any breakfast.

The old man drove through the forest, but when he came to the pine on the hill his daughters were lying there dead. He picked them up, put them at the bottom of the sledge with their faces covered, and drove sorrowfully home. Their mother ran out to see what rich gifts they had brought with them.

'Where are the girls?' she shouted.

'In the sledge behind me.'

She lifted the covers and found them lying dead. In a fury she started shrieking abuse at her husband. 'What have you done, you old fool? You have destroyed my daughters – my pigeons, my own red cherries! I will thrash you with the poker! I will beat you with the stove-rake!'

Then the old man spoke up for the first time in his life.

'That's enough. You thought those girls were going to get rich, and they might have done well enough if they had been as gentle and soft-spoken as my Marfa. Besides – who sent them out into the forest?'

And his wife for once was silenced.

As for Marfa, she married a handsome young man from the village and they lived happily. But when their children get quarrelsome or are rude, the old man frightens them with stories about Frost.

ЦАРЕВНА-ЛАГ҃КА·

THE FROG TSAREVNA

A LONG, long time ago, far away over the steppes and the rivers and the forests, there lived a tsar who had three young sons. All of them were brave and handsome, but the bravest and most handsome was the youngest, Tsarevich Ivan.

One day the Tsar called them to him and said: 'My dear sons, it is time that you married; I wish to see my children's children before I die. Take your bows into that field over there. No one has been allowed to hunt over it, and I want each of you to choose a direction and shoot an arrow. Follow your arrow and wherever it falls go and look for your bride.'

So the tsareviches took their bows to the field, and they shot their arrows. The eldest brother turned to the east and shot, the second to the west, but Tsarevich Ivan drew his bow with all his strength and shot his arrow straight in front of him.

The eldest brother found that his arrow had fallen in the courtyard of a nobleman, right in front of the apartments where his daughter lived. The second had managed to shoot his through the window of a rich merchant's daughter. But Tsarevich Ivan's arrow could not be found at all.

For two whole days he wandered in the woods and fields looking for it, and then on the third day he came by chance to a marsh where the boggy ground gave way below his feet. There in the middle sat a huge frog, and in her mouth she was holding his arrow.

When he saw this he knew there was magic, and he turned to run away. But the frog called: 'Brek-kek-kex! Tsarevich Ivan, come here and fetch your arrow and take me to be your bride. If you do not, you will never get out of this swamp.'

Trembling, Ivan made his way over the quaking, treacherous ground, picked up the frog and took the arrow. Then with much sadness he made his way home. When he arrived at the palace his brothers jeered at him, and their two beautiful brides mocked him too, so that he went sorrowfully to the Tsar and said: 'How can I marry an object like this, that croaks brek-kek-kex? Marriage is not like just fording a river or crossing a field. How can I live with a frog?'

But the Tsar said: 'You must take her, for that was my royal word and that is your destiny.'

So the Tsar's three sons were married – the eldest to a nobleman's daughter, the second to a merchant's daughter, and the third, Tsarevich Ivan, to the frog. They set up their separate establishments, and Tsarevich Ivan treated the frog with kindness and gentleness.

Then one day the Tsar called his three sons and said: 'Dear children, I should like to try the skill of my daughters-in-law. So each of you go to my store room and take a piece of linen. Give it to your wife and tell her to make me a shirt by tomorrow morning.'

The two elder brothers took the linen to their respective wives who at once called all their maid-servants, and set to cutting out the stuff and sewing it. As they stitched they laughed to think how Tsarevich Ivan's frog wife was going to manage. And Tsarevich Ivan himself was full of woe, and went back home with hanging head. 'Of course I am sad,' he said to the frog when she asked him the reason. 'The Tsar my father has set a task that I know is beyond your strength.'

'Koax, koax,' she croaked. 'Have no fear. Go to bed and rest. Everyone is wiser in the morning than in the evening.' And when the Tsarevich had left her she told her servants to cut the linen into small pieces. They obeyed and went away. Then she took the pieces in her mouth, hopped over to the window, flung them out and said: 'Winds! Winds! Fly with these pieces and sew me a shirt for the Tsar.' And almost before she had said this a shirt, all stitched and finished, came flying back into the room.

Next morning she gave it to the Tsarevich, and he, delighted, put it under his coat and took it to the palace where his brothers had already arrived. The eldest presented his shirt first. The Tsar was scornful. 'It might do for one of my servants who wasn't very particular,' he said, tossing it down. Then he took the shirt which the merchant's daughter had stitched. 'A little better,' he said. 'I might possibly wear it to the bath-house on a dark day.'

But when he took the shirt that Tsarevich Ivan offered him he was delighted. Not a single seam could be seen in it, and he gave instructions that it should be kept for wearing only on state occasions. Ivan went home well pleased. But his brothers said to each other: 'That wife of his is not a frog but a witch.'

The Tsar then devised a second test. Again he called his three sons, and this time he told them that he wanted their wives to bake him some bread. 'Each of you must bring me a loaf of soft white bread tomorrow morning, and then we shall be able to see which of your brides is a true housewife.'

Tsarevich Ivan went home with a long face, and seeing him the frog said: 'Brek-kek-kek koax koax. Why are you so sad? Has your father the Tsar used you harshly?' And when he told her of the task that had been set she was still cheerful. 'Go to bed and sleep,' she told him. 'You will be wiser in the morning.'

When he was asleep she ordered her servants to make a

paste of flour and water and to put it into the cold oven. Then she hopped to the oven door and said:

> 'Bread, bread, baker's dough,
> Bake yourself as white as snow!'

The oven door flew open and there was the loaf cooked to a turn, white and soft inside, golden brown on the outside. What was more, it was prettily decorated with the design of a city – domes and towers and gateways.

Now the two other Tsarevnas hated the frog because her shirt had been so much finer than theirs, and they ordered an old hen-wife to spy on her to see how she baked her loaf. When the old woman told them what she had seen and heard, they ordered flour and water to be brought, mixed it, poured the paste into cold ovens and repeated the spell. But nothing happened. The paste just dripped all over the ovens and stayed uncooked. So in a fury they had to send for more flour, and this time they used yeast and hot water and heated the ovens in the usual way. Even this didn't work, for the paste had clogged the flues. So one loaf was burnt black and the other half-cooked.

Next morning the three sons presented their loaves. The Tsar flung aside the first offering. 'You can take that to the kitchen and give it to the beggars at the door,' he said scornfully. He was scarcely less contemptuous when he tasted the second loaf. 'It might do for my hounds,' was all he could say.

Last of all, Tsarevich Ivan unwrapped his bread. And when he saw it his father was at a loss for words. For the loaf was so splendid that it seemed to come out of a fairy tale. And what was more, it was delicious to eat. The Tsar tasted it and said that it must be kept for Easter Sunday. So the Tsarevich went home rejoicing.

But the Tsar had a third test for the young wives. Again he sent for his sons. This time he said: 'It is fitting that all women of the nobility should be able to weave and

embroider in gold and silver. So all three of you go to my treasury and take silk, gold and silver, and bring me a carpet in the morning.'

When the frog saw the Tsarevich Ivan come in with slow and heavy tread and downcast face she said: 'Brek kek kek kex, koax koax. What is it now? Has your father been so very cruel?' And when he told her of the new task she was still cheerful. 'Go and sleep. The day brings more wisdom than the night.'

As soon as she saw he was safely asleep she ordered her

servants to cut the silk and the silver and gold thread into
small pieces. Then as before she threw the pieces out of the
window.

'Winds! Winds! fly with these pieces and make me a carpet
such as my dear father used to cover his windows!' And
scarcely had she said the words before the embroidered
carpet came flying through the window.

Now the other Tsarevnas had once again sent the hen-wife
to spy on the frog, and when she told them what she had seen
they could not believe that the spell would not work this
time. So they cut all their precious materials into pieces and
threw them out of the window. They waited a long time,
but the winds sent them no carpets. So they beat the poor
hen-wife savagely, sent for more materials, made all their
maids sit down with them, and they wove and stitched all
night.

But in the morning when he saw the result the Tsar shook
his head at the waste of fine materials. 'Send this carpet out
to the stable,' he said to his eldest son, 'it might do as a horse
blanket.' And to the second son he said: 'Put your wife's
carpet on the hall floor by the door; the servants can wipe
their feet on it.' Then the Tsarevich Ivan unrolled his carpet,
and the Tsar was awestruck. It was not only the most
beautiful design he had ever seen, but it seemed to have been
woven by fairy hands. And the Tsar decreed that it should be
put in his treasury and only brought out on solemn
feast-days.

'Now, my dear children,' he said, 'your wives have done all

that I asked them to do. Bring them to dine with me tomorrow and let us celebrate.'

The two older brothers went home rejoicing. 'However clever that other one is,' they said to each other, 'she is only a frog, and everyone will see and laugh her to scorn.' But the Tsarevich Ivan came back in despair. 'You have made the shirt, and baked the bread, and woven the carpet,' he said to his wife. 'But in the end you are only a frog, and my sisters-in-law are beautiful women. How can I hold up my head in front of them all?'

'Koax, koax,' said the frog. 'Never fear. You sleep and see what wisdom the morning will bring.'

When he woke in the morning she said: 'Have faith. The Tsar your father was pleased with the shirt I made, and with the bread and the carpet. Perhaps he will be pleased with your wife too. You go to the palace and I will follow later. Make your respects to the Tsar, and when you hear a rumbling and a knocking say: "Here comes my poor little frog in her box!" Then you will see what you will see.' So Ivan departed for the palace a little cheered.

When he was out of sight, the frog went to the window and called: 'Winds! Winds! Bring me a carriage with six white horses and outriders and postilions!'

Instantly a horn blew and horsemen came galloping up, followed by six white horses drawing a golden coach. And the frog threw off her skin and grew into a princess of such beauty that it cannot be described by any pen.

Meanwhile the company was gathering at the palace, and

there were the two older brothers with their lovely brides finely dressed in silks, and decked with jewels. They jeered at Ivan, standing by himself: 'Why did you not bring your Tsarevna, Ivan? You could have dressed her in a dish clout. Are you sure you chose the greatest beauty in the swamp?'

Then there was a sound of horses approaching, and rumbling wheels. 'Do not be startled,' said Tsarevich Ivan. 'It is only my poor frog in her box.' But everybody rushed to the windows, and outside they saw outriders galloping, followed by a splendid golden coach drawn by six milk-white horses. And when the coach drew up, out stepped a princess of such beauty that she put the sun and the moon to shame.

She came up to Tsarevich Ivan, who led her to his father, and the Tsar took her by the hand and sat her beside him. As everyone began to feast and be merry her sisters-in-law eyed her jealously. 'It is as we thought,' they whispered to each other. 'She is a witch. We must watch her carefully and do all that she does.' And when they saw that she did not drink the dregs of her wine but poured them into her left sleeve, and that she put the bones of her roast swan into her right sleeve, they did the same.

When they rose up from the table the musicians began to play, and the Tsar led out Ivan's beautiful bride to dance, which she did with great grace. As she danced she waved her left sleeve, and at one end of the banquet hall a lake appeared. Then she waved her right sleeve and swans and geese were seen swimming on it. When she had finished

dancing the lake and the fowls on it disappeared. The Tsar and his guests marvelled.

Then her sisters-in-law began to dance. They waved their left sleeves and all the guests were splashed with wine dregs; they waved their right sleeves and swan bones flew around; one even hit the Tsar in the eye. He was angry and ordered the two wives out of the palace, and they went home shamefaced.

But Tsarevich Ivan worried in case his beautiful wife should turn into a frog again. So while everyone else was dancing he hurried home, searched till he found the frog-skin, and then threw it in the fire. When his wife came home and could not find it she realized what he had done. Then she began weeping and said: 'Alas, alas, Tsarevich Ivan. Why could you not have had more patience? I am a fairy, Vassilissa the Wise. Now you have lost me for ever, unless you can find me beyond three times nine lands, in the thirtieth tsardom, in the empire that lies under the sun.'

Tsarevich Ivan wept bitter tears. Then he prayed to God, said farewell to the Tsar his father and the Tsarina his mother, and went in search of his wife.

He went on and on, but a tale is told far more swiftly than a journey is made. He travelled through three times nine lands, asking everyone he met where he could find Vassilissa the Wise. But no one could tell him, until he reached the empire that lies under the sun, and there he met an old, old man to whom he told his story.

'Yes, I know Vassilissa the Wise,' said the old man. 'She is a fairy, the daughter of the wicked Kashchey the Deathless, and her father, in a fit of anger, turned her into a frog for three years. This time was almost up, and if you had not burnt her frog-skin she would be with you now. I cannot tell you where she is, but take this magic ball, which will roll wherever you tell it. Follow that.'

The Tsarevich thanked the old man, threw the ball on the ground, and it immediately began to roll. It rolled and rolled, across a stony plain, and into a dark, dreary forest. There in the middle he came to a miserable little hut that stood on hen's legs and turned round all the time. Ivan said to it:

> 'Little hut, little hut,
> Stand the way your mother placed you,
> Turn your back to the wood,
> Turn your front to me.'

And immediately the hut stood still and turned to face him.

Tsarevich Ivan climbed up one of its hen's legs and went in. And there he saw the oldest of the Baba Yagas, the bony grandmother of all witches, lying on a corner of the stove on nine bricks, with one lip on the shelf, and her nose (which was as long as a bridge) thrust up the chimney. Her huge iron mortar was in the corner.

She gnashed her teeth and shouted at him. 'Until now I have never seen or heard the spirit of any Russian, but today a Russian has come into my house. Well, Tsarevich Ivan, did you come of your own will, or because someone else forced you?'

'Partly by my own will, partly by force,' said young Ivan. 'But for shame, you have not offered me food and drink, nor a bath!'

The Baba Yaga was pleased with his boldness, put food and drink before him, and prepared him a bath. Then he told her his story. When she heard that Vassilissa the Wise was indeed his wife, she said: 'I will help you, not for love of you, but because I hate her father, Kashchey the Deathless. You will have to destroy him first, and you will see how difficult that is going to be when I tell you that his life is not carried in his own body. He has hidden it away at the point of a needle, the needle is in an egg, the egg is in a duck, the duck is in a hare, the hare is in a stone casket, and the casket is high up on the top of an oak tree a long way off. And Kashchey has ringed the tree with enchantment.'

But young Ivan refused to be daunted, and slept well that night. The next morning he set the ball rolling and journeyed behind it. He rode a long way, too long to be told in a tale, and in one of the dark forests through which he had to make his way he came across a great bear whose paw was caught beneath a fallen tree. He drew his sword and cut away the branches, and the bear went free. A little further on he saw a fox caught in a snare. He released the fox, but nearby he

found a hawk struggling in a tangle of vines. So he freed that too before he went on.

At last, after many days of journeying, he came to the shores of a sea. And there, gasping out its life, lay a stranded pike-fish. Pitying it, the Tsarevich dismounted from his horse and threw it back into the sea. And then, turning, he saw the tall oak tree, and could just make out the stone casket at the top of it. But he would have to be a bird to fly up there.

As he was straining his eyes to see the casket, and pondering what to do, the bear that he had helped came rushing out of the woods and knocked the tree down. The casket fell from among the branches, burst open and a hare sprang out and scampered off. But the fox that Ivan had saved ran after it, caught it and tore it to pieces. From the hare flew a duck, but now the hawk appeared and darted into the sky after it. The duck dropped an egg, and the egg fell into the sea.

At this sight Ivan felt that everything was lost, but as he stood weeping, the pike came swimming to the shore with the egg in its mouth. As the Tsarevich took it in his hand there was the sound of whistling wind, and Kashchey, green-eyed, naked and hairy, with a bared sword in his hand and a nose curved like a scimitar, stood there, grinding his teeth and spitting with rage. But he grew pale as Ivan squeezed the egg, and shook violently as the prince tossed the egg from one hand to another. He writhed and screamed as the egg's shell was broken and the needle was taken out, then fell on his knees as Tsarevich Ivan struggled and tried to break off its point. At last it snapped and Kashchey fell down dead.

The Tsarevich made a great pyre and burnt the body of the sorcerer and scattered the ashes to the winds. Then, still led by the magic ball, he walked away from the sea-shore till he came to Kashchey's palace. And there Vassilissa the Wise, his Tsarevna, came down the steps to meet him, no longer a frog but the most beautiful princess that ever walked this earth.

So he put her on his horse and they rode back to his own country, where they lived a long and happy life.

SALT

LONG ago, in a distant land, there lived a rich merchant. He traded with many countries, and owned a large fleet of ships which he sent here, there, and everywhere. He had three sons. Two of them were capable and prudent like their father, but the youngest was known as Ivan the Fool because he never seemed to be able to behave like a sensible being. If there was anything stupid to do you can be sure Ivan would go and do it.

When the boys grew up their father decided to let them try their hands at business too. So he sent the two elder ones off, each in a ship laden with furs, fine linen, gold and silver goods, embroidered carpets. They were to sell these cargoes to foreign customers and come back rich men.

But he knew that his youngest son could not be trusted with such responsibility. So Ivan the Fool saw his brothers sail away to make their fortunes, and for the first time in his life he wished that he was more like them. He went to his father and kissed his hand and begged for a ship too so that he could seek his fortune.

'You!' said his father. 'But you're always playing the giddy goat – you've never done anything serious in your life.'

'I know,' said Ivan. 'But that's all over now and I'm going

to try my hand at being wise. Just try me with a ship, little father, and you'll see what I can do.'

'There must be an old ship in your fleet that you could spare,' begged his mother.

'Very well,' said his father, 'only I'm not going to throw good money after bad by putting a cargo in it.'

So he found a little old ship and a crew of old, old sailors who were past work, and instead of cargo he filled the hold with rags and rubbish as ballast. Ivan the Fool went on board, the ancient, tottering sailors managed to hoist the ragged sails and weigh the anchor, and they sailed on the tide, off away on the high seas to seek their fortune.

At first the winds were fair, but on the third day there came a fearful storm that battered them until they thought they must surely sink. The sails were all carried away, and when at last the wind died down they found they had been flung up on the shores of an island that was not marked on their maps and charts. Ivan looked at his battered little ship.

'Well, my children,' he said to his sailors, 'we've got to have more sails, that's for sure. We'll just have to do the best we can with the rags in the hold. You get on with that and I'll take a look at the island and see what I can find.'

So the old sailors staggered to and fro carrying out the bales of rags and sorting through them. Then they settled down on the shore and stitched and patched them together. Meanwhile, Ivan went off walking inland. In the distance was a high mountain which seemed to be covered with snow from head to foot even though it was midsummer and the sun was blazing down. There was nothing growing on it, it was just white, white all the way down. Ivan was feeling thirsty in all that heat, so he picked up some of the snow and crammed it in his mouth. Then he quickly spat it out. It was not snow – it was salt. He ran back to the shore where his ship was now floating on the tide.

'Empty the holds and sweep them clean,' he shouted to the old men who were now scrambling up the masts with the sails they had contrived. 'I've got a new cargo that will make our fortune.' Then, hour after hour, grumbling and swearing, the crew went to and fro between the mountain and ship, carrying sackfuls of salt and stowing it away below deck. At last, when their backs were nearly breaking and there was no room for even a grain more, Ivan gave the orders to put off, and away they sailed.

After many days on an empty sea, they saw land on the horizon, and the towers and walls of a town. They knew that where there is a town there is a harbour, and they were right. They sailed in and made their ship fast. Ivan left his men and went ashore, taking with him a little bag of salt. 'You never know, it might be useful,' he said to himself.

There was a palace above the harbour, with golden domes, and the people in the street told him that it belonged to the Tsar. So in he went and asked for audience. He had to wait, for many other people had come to petition the Tsar. Then, when his turn came he stepped forward boldly and held out his bag of salt.

'And what is that?' said the Tsar.

'Salt,' said Ivan. 'I have a cargo of it in the hold of my ship, and I want to trade it in this country.'

'Salt?' said the Tsar, 'what is that?' Then he looked into the bag and gave a loud laugh. 'It's nothing but white dust. You must be a fool if you think that you can sell us that!'

This was too near what his family had always said. Mortified, Ivan bowed and left. But outside the audience chamber he thought again. 'It doesn't sound as if these people had ever heard of salt,' he said to himself, and he went round to the palace kitchen to see what they put in their food.

In the kitchen cooks and scullions were scurrying to and fro preparing the Tsar's dinner. Ivan sat on a stool in a corner to keep out of their way but watched them closely. They were roasting, and boiling, and frying, and rolling out pastry, and kneading dough, but never a grain of salt went into any of the food, not even into the potatoes. Ivan watched his moment, and when they went out of the room to get the tables ready in the banqueting hall, he slipped off the stool and ran to the stoves and put salt from his bag into all the saucepans. Then he opened the oven doors and sprinkled the meat inside with salt too. 'Now it will taste better,' he told himself with satisfaction; the thought of the unsalted food had made him feel ill.

In ran all the servants, put the food on to gold plates and carried it away. In the hall the Tsar, his wife the Tsarina, and their daughter the Tsarevna marvelled at how good the food tasted; the soup and the fish and the meat all had a flavour they had never known before. The cooks were summoned and asked to account for it.

'What did you put into the food that you have never put before?' demanded the Tsar. 'Will you be able to do it again?'

But the cooks stared at each other. They didn't know.

'Little father, we did as we always have done,' said the head cook at last. 'There was no change that we know of.'

So the scullions were brought in and questioned, but they had noticed nothing different either. Then one of them remembered Ivan. 'If you please, little father, usually we allow no one in the kitchen. But today there was a young Russian merchant who said he wanted to study our style of cooking. He sat in a corner and was no trouble to anyone – he just watched us.'

The Tsar commanded that Ivan should be brought, and in he came with his bag of salt. 'Did you do anything to the food?' thundered the Tsar.

Ivan trembled, but he looked the Tsar in the eye and spoke up boldly. 'I put salt into every dish,' he said.

'That white dust you showed me?' said the Tsar incredulously.

'The same.'

'Have you got any more of it?'

'I have got a ship in the harbour that is laden with nothing else,' said Ivan proudly.

'Then I will buy every grain you have. What do you want for it?'

'Well,' said Ivan, 'since it's you I'll make a reduction. For every bag of salt you can give me one of gold, one of precious stones, and one of silver.'

'Fair enough,' said the Tsar, 'for a dust that is magic.' And he commanded that the salt should be carried to his treasury.

So all through the day and through the night the old sailors toiled up to the palace with bags of salt, and carried bags of gold, silver and precious stones down to the ship. They stowed what they could in the hold, and the rest they made fast on deck. Then exhausted, they lay down and slept.

In the morning they found the beautiful young Tsarevna standing on the quay with her nurses and maids. She was staring curiously at the little old ship with its patchwork sails. 'What a strange ship! I've never seen anything like it,' she said.

'Would you like to come on board?' said Ivan. And he showed her everything, and told her what the different sails and masts and the parts of the ship were called. He told her too that when Russian sailors hauled up the anchor, which was very heavy work, they sang sea-shanties to help them along.

'Oh I would like to hear that!' said the Tsarevna.

So Ivan gave orders to his crew, the old men sang in their cracked voices as they turned the capstan and wound up the anchor, and the little ship slipped out of the harbour. When the Tsarevna at last looked back to see what was happening, the towers and domes of her father's palace were just a gleam on the horizon.

At first she cried, but Ivan was kind and gentle and talked

to her so delightfully that she soon dried her eyes and began to enjoy herself. He told her that he was on his way back to his father's country and asked her to marry him when they arrived there, and she agreed.

After they had sailed for many days they saw on the horizon two splendid ships with big white sails – ships very different from their own weather-beaten little craft with its sails cobbled together from rags. 'Those are my brothers' ships,' said Ivan joyfully, and as they drew near he hailed them and called his brothers to come on board and meet his bride.

At first his two elders fell about with laughing as they pointed out to each other the shabbiness of everything and the crew of old men in their ragged clothes, but then they saw the bags of treasure and the radiant young Tsarevna and they muttered among themselves.

'What is Ivan the Fool doing with all this?' said one.

'Scuttle him,' said the other.

So that evening, after there had been drinking and merry-making on board to celebrate the reunion, the two older brothers crept up behind Ivan as he stood on deck and tipped him over the side. They shed many tears in the morning when he could not be found, and it was agreed that he must have fallen overboard, and that the brothers had better take the ship with its treasure and the Tsarevna into their care.

But Ivan was not drowned as they thought. He was clinging on to a large log and watching the ships sail away into the distance. After a bit he managed to climb on to the

log, and there he sat for several days drifting and hoping that
a ship would pick him up. No ship did come, but just as he
was getting too weak to sit there much longer, the log was
washed up on a sandy shore, and he staggered out of the
water and fell asleep.

When the light woke him in the morning, he had a terrible
fright. He was lying outside a house that looked as big as a
mountain, and as he stared at it the door opened and a giant
came striding out.

'And just who may you be?' roared the giant. 'You're on
private land – be off with you!'

Ivan managed to tell his story. The giant listened, and at
the end he said: 'That's a sad tale, and there's sadder to come.
I can tell you what has happened since your brothers got
home. The elder one is going to marry your princess tomorrow, and there's going to be a splendid wedding feast. But
don't fret; I can get you there in time.'

And he picked up Ivan, set him on his shoulders, and
strode through the sea at a furious rate – a verst at each step.
Sometimes the water came up to his armpits, and Ivan on his
shoulders became drenched with spray. Then they reached
dry land again and the giant set him down.

'Now run along and you'll be in time,' he told him. 'But
mind, not a word about who's brought you here. If you ever
dare talk about this ride you'll regret it. I warn you, I'll be
able to hear you ten thousand versts off.'

Ivan promised to be silent, and then hurried off to his
father's house. He found that the wedding feast had begun,

and there sitting round the top table were his parents and his second brother, and in the place of honour his eldest brother and the Tsarevna whom he was about to marry. Everyone was flushed with wine and in excellent spirits, except the young princess, and she was tense and pale. As Ivan strode through the room she stood up and called: 'This is the man I pledged my hand to – not this liar and cheat beside me.'

And when the merchant heard the story he turned his two elder sons out of the house, giving their ships and all their possessions to Ivan. So the wedding feast started all over again, but this time Ivan sat in the place of honour, with his Tsarevna beside him. More wine was sent for and the guests refilled their goblets again and again. People became boastful and told loud stories about their wealth or their strength or their skill at hunting, and Ivan became weary of all their bragging.

'I can tell you one thing,' he said, 'I am the only man here who has ridden to this wedding on the shoulders of a giant.'

Instantly the ground shook as if there was an earthquake, and there was a huge eye looking through one of the windows.

'Little man,' roared the giant in a voice that made the house rock, 'didn't I warn you to keep your mouth shut!'

'Forgive me,' said Ivan, 'it was the drink that was boasting, not I.'

'What sort of drink is it that makes a man boast?' asked the giant.

'Try it for yourself,' said Ivan, and he ordered the servants to roll the largest barrel of wine in his father's cellar into the courtyard, and then one of beer the same size, and another of mead. There was enough in each for a hundred men, but the giant picked them up one after the other as if they were thimbles and swallowed every drop. Then he began roaring and stamping and lurching around so that it was lucky the house didn't get crushed under his feet, though a lot of others did. At last he fell flat on his back and slept for three days and three nights, surrounded by wreckage.

'Look at what you've done,' said Ivan when he woke at last.

'And that was just because of that tiny drop of drink?' said the giant, staring blearily around him. 'Well, if drink can make a man do that, you can boast about me for a thousand years and I won't lift a finger.' Still staggering a little, he went down to the sea and strode off into it.

And Ivan (no one ever called him a fool again) and his princess lived in perfect happiness for many long years.

СКАЗКА
ОБЪ
Иванѣ-царевичѣ,
Жаръ-птицѣ и
о сѣромъ волкѣ.

TSAREVICH IVAN, THE FIREBIRD
AND THE GREY WOLF

FAR away and long ago there lived a Tsar called Demyan
who had three sons – Tsarevich Dimitri, Tsarevich Vassily and Tsarevich Ivan.

Now, this Tsar had a most beautiful garden; there was not
one like it anywhere else in the world. There were many rare
trees in it, trees that bore jewels rather than fruit, but the
rarest of all was an apple tree whose apples were made of pure
gold. And this was the tree that the Tsar loved best.

One day he saw to his great grief that a golden apple was
missing. He set guards on all the gates into the garden, but in

spite of this, each morning he found that another apple had gone. At last he stationed sentries on the walls, and it was these men who saw what happened. Every night, they said, a bird came flying into the garden. It was a most wonderful bird that shone like fire, with golden feathers and eyes like crystal, and it would perch on the apple tree, pick a golden apple and fly away.

The Tsar vowed that this must stop. He called his two eldest sons and said: 'Whichever of you shall catch this thieving Firebird and bring it to me alive, shall have half my tsardom, and shall rule after me when I am dead.' And the two sons both shouted joyfully that they would not fail to capture the bird and bring it to him.

Tsarevich Dimitri and Tsarevich Vassily cast lots to see who should be the first to try his luck, and Tsarevich Dimitri won. So, in the evening he went into the garden and sat down under the apple tree. He watched until midnight, but then he fell asleep. In the morning the Tsar said to him: 'Well, my son, did you see this Firebird?' Tsarevich Dimitri was ashamed to tell the truth. He said: 'No, Sire. I watched all night, but the Firebird did not come.' But when the Tsar went to the tree to count the apples he found that one had gone.

The next night it was Tsarevich Vassily's turn. He watched until midnight then he too fell asleep. When his father asked him whether he had seen the thief, he was ashamed – just like his brother – to admit that he had slept, and he said: 'Sire, I did not close my eyes. No bird came into your garden last night.' But again when Tsar Demyan

counted the apples he found that another had been taken.

On the third evening Tsarevich Ivan asked if he might keep watch. His father loved the boy and was afraid the task was beyond his strength, especially as his older brothers had failed. But young Ivan pleaded with him, and at last Tsar Demyan gave way. So when night fell he sat under the apple tree with its golden fruit. By the time midnight approached he felt his eyes getting heavy, but he grasped his dagger and pressed the point into his thigh until the pain drove away sleep. Then, an hour after midnight, he saw the garden become as bright as if it were on fire; he heard a clattering of wings, and there on the lowest branch of the tree perched a glowing bird, its beak outstretched to pluck an apple.

Tsarevich Ivan crept near, and then sprang towards the bird and seized its tail. But the bird, beating with its golden wings, tore itself loose and flew away, leaving the boy holding a single golden feather. He wrapped it in his handkerchief, and lay down and went to sleep.

The next morning his father called him and said: 'Dear son, I suppose you too failed to see the Firebird?' Then Tsarevich Ivan unrolled the handkerchief and there was the dazzling feather, shining brighter than a hundred candles. The Tsar marvelled, took it and put it in his treasury, and set many watchmen in the garden, hoping to catch the bird. But it did not return.

The Tsar could not get it out of his mind. He would stare at the feather and long to see the wonderful creature it came from. At last he said to his eldest sons: 'Take your horses and go in search of this Firebird. I will give half my tsardom to the one who brings it to me alive.' Tsarevich Dimitri and Tsarevich Vassily, envious of their brother Ivan, were glad that their father had not asked him to go too, and they saddled their horses and went off on their quest.

They rode on and on. Whether it was a long time or a short time no one can say, for a tale is told long before a journey is over. At last they came to a green plain where three roads met. And there at the crossroads they saw a stone with these words carved on it:

> Who rides straight forward shall meet both hunger and cold.
> Who rides to the right shall live though his horse shall die.
> Who rides to the left shall die, though his horse shall live.

None of these routes seemed very promising, so the young men turned aside into a pleasant wood, pitched their tents, and settled down to a life of ease, forgetting why they had come.

At home the weeks and the months went by and still there was no word from the brothers. Tsarevich Ivan became restless and begged his father to let him go out after them. But Tsar Demyan did not want to lose him too: 'You are so young,' he said, 'far too young for such an ordeal. And I am old. If God takes my life and you too are gone, who will there be to keep order in the tsardom? Stay with me.'

But Tsarevich Ivan went on pleading, and at last his father gave way. The young man chose a swift horse and set off. On and on he rode, until he reached the green plain where three roads met. There he read the inscription on the stone. 'If I take the left road I will die,' he said to himself. 'And on the middle road I will have to face hunger and cold. So I will take the one that goes to the right, even though my poor horse may be lost.'

So off he went. He rode and he rode, and on the morning of the fourth day, as he led his horse through a forest, a huge grey wolf leapt out at them. 'You're a brave lad, Tsarevich Ivan,' said the Wolf, 'but didn't you read what was on the stone?' And he sprang on the horse, tore it into pieces, devoured it, and disappeared.

The Tsarevich wept for his horse, and stumbled on through the forest on foot. He was nearly fainting with weariness when again he met the Grey Wolf. 'I said you were a brave lad, Tsarevich Ivan,' said the Wolf, 'and for this reason I'll take pity on you now. I have eaten your horse and I owe you something. Sit on my back and tell me where you want to be taken.'

So Tsarevich Ivan sat on the Wolf's back. 'Grey Wolf,' he said, 'take me to the Firebird that stole my father's apples.' Off went the Wolf, faster than the fastest horse. They forded rushing rivers, they swept through forests, and did not stop until they reached a stone wall.

'Climb over this wall, Tsarevich Ivan,' said the Wolf. 'On the other side you will find a garden, and in the garden there is an iron railing. Behind the railing are three cages, one of copper, one of silver, one of gold. In the copper cage there is a crow, in the silver one a jackdaw, but in the golden cage

you will find the Firebird. Open the door of the cage, take out the Firebird and wrap it in your handkerchief. But whatever you do, don't be tempted to take the golden cage.'

Tsarevich Ivan climbed the wall, and found it was just as the Wolf had said. So over the railing he went, and there were the three cages. He opened the door of the golden one and took out the Firebird. But the cage was so beautiful he could not bear to leave it behind. Besides, he thought, he might need it to carry the bird. The minute that he picked it up there was a deafening noise of clanging bells and twanging musical instruments, and watchmen came rushing into the garden. They seized Tsarevich Ivan and tied him up, and in the morning they brought him before their Tsar, who was called Dolmat.

Tsar Dolmat was in a fine state of fury. 'And just who are you, and what do you think you're doing in my garden, trying to steal my property?'

'I am the son of Tsar Demyan,' said Tsarevich Ivan, 'and my name is Ivan. The Firebird used to come into my father's garden and pluck his golden apples, and my father sent me in search of the thief.'

'How do I know that you're not lying?' shouted Tsar Dolmat. 'If you had come to me first and told your story I might have given you the bird. But now I'll blazon your name far and wide so everybody will know of your crime. Only one thing will save you. If you ride across three times nine countries to the thirtieth tsardom of Tsar Afron and take the Horse with the Golden Mane which his father promised me and which rightly belongs to me, then you can have the Firebird. If you fail I'll see to it that the whole world knows of your disgraceful behaviour.'

Tsarevich Ivan departed, full of grief. He found the Grey Wolf and told his story.

'You're a foolish boy,' said the Grey Wolf. 'Why didn't you listen to what I told you?'

'I am guilty before you,' said Tsarevich Ivan sadly.

'Well,' said the Grey Wolf, 'I will help you again. Get on my back and tell me where to go.'

So for a second time Tsarevich Ivan sat on the Wolf's back. 'Take me across three times nine countries to the thirtieth tsardom of Tsar Afron, to the Horse with the Golden Mane.'

And the Wolf began running. Rivers and forests didn't stop him, he went through them like an arrow, and by the time the next night fell he had reached Tsar Afron's palace and the royal stables.

'Now, Tsarevich Ivan,' said the Wolf, 'the stablemen are all asleep. Go and take the Horse with the Golden Mane. But be sure not to touch the golden bridle on the wall or terrible things will happen.'

So Tsarevich Ivan opened the stable door and there in a blaze of light stood the Horse with the Golden Mane. He seized its halter, but as he was leading it out he saw the golden bridle, which was so beautiful that he could not resist taking it down from the wall. At once there was a great clanging, for the bridle was bound by invisible cords to brass instruments, and the noise woke all the stablemen. They swarmed round him and tied him up, and in the morning he was taken before Tsar Afron.

'You look like a boy of good family,' said the Tsar. 'Not at all the sort of lad to be skulking round trying to take other people's property. Who is your father, eh? Does he know about all this?'

'My father is Tsar Demyan,' said young Ivan, 'of the tsardom of Demyan. But it was Tsar Dolmat who told me to bring him the Horse with the Golden Mane. He says it is rightly his.'

'If you had come and asked me in his name then I would have given you the horse,' said the Tsar. 'As it is you are no better than a common thief, and this is what I shall tell my heralds to proclaim throughout the length and the breadth of all the tsardoms, including your father's. There is only one way you can save yourself. You must ride over three times nine kingdoms to the land of the tsar whose daughter is known as Elena the Beautiful and bring her to be my bride. I have loved her with all my heart and soul but I have never been able to win her. If you do this I'll forgive you, and you can have the Horse with the Golden Mane and the golden bridle for Tsar Dolmat. If not I'll see to it that everyone knows what you have tried to do – and failed.'

Tsarevich Ivan left the palace in a great state of grief and told the Grey Wolf what had happened.

'The folly of it!' lamented the Wolf. 'Why can you never remember what I tell you?'

'Grey Wolf,' said Tsarevich Ivan, weeping, 'I am guilty before you.'

'Well,' said the Grey Wolf, 'we must try again. Sit on my back. Where do you want to go now?'

For the third time the Tsarevich Ivan climbed on the Wolf. 'Take me across three times nine lands to the tsarevna who is called Elena the Beautiful.' Off the Wolf streaked, and rivers and forests gave him no more trouble than a puddle or a stick in the path. At last he stopped at a golden railing with a beautiful garden beyond it.

'Get down now, Tsarevich Ivan,' said the Grey Wolf. 'Go back along the road we came by, and wait for me under the oak tree in the field.'

So the Tsarevich did as he was told. And the Grey Wolf

lurked by the railing. Then in the cool of the evening when the sun was low, the Tsar's daughter, Elena the Beautiful, came out to walk with her nurses and her ladies in waiting. When she drew near, the Grey Wolf suddenly leapt from the shadows, seized her and sped off. He ran back to the field where the Tsarevich Ivan was waiting under the oak tree.

'Mount on my back, Tsarevich Ivan,' said the Wolf, 'and take the Tsarevna in your arms.' And off he ran, swifter than fire, swifter than a lightning flash, across the three times nine tsardoms, back to the tsardom of Tsar Afron. The nurses and the ladies in waiting had gone running back to the palace to tell the Tsarevna's father what had happened, but none of the horses in his tsardom could outpace the Grey Wolf.

Sitting on the Wolf with the Tsarevna in his arms, Tsarevich Ivan could only think of how much he loved her. And she, recovering from her fright, began to love him too. So that when they reached the country of Tsar Afron, Tsarevich Ivan began to weep at the thought of parting with her.

'I am in love with Elena the Beautiful,' he told the Grey Wolf. 'And now I must give her up to Tsar Afron in return for the Horse with the Golden Mane. For if I do not my name will be dishonoured for ever.'

'We have gone through a lot together,' said the Grey Wolf, 'and I may as well help once more. Listen. When we come to the palace, I myself will take on the shape of the Tsarevna, and you shall lead me to Tsar Afron, hand me over, and take in exchange the Horse with the Golden Mane. Mount him and ride off. Then I, the false Tsarevna, will ask leave to walk

upon the steppe, and when I am out there with the court ladies, you have only to think of me, the Grey Wolf, and I shall join you.'

As the Wolf spoke he beat his paw on the ground, and instantly he took on the shape of the Tsarevna – so like her, indeed, that no one could have told the difference. Then, telling the real Elena the Beautiful to wait for him outside, Tsarevich Ivan led the false one to Tsar Afron. The Tsar was delighted to have won this treasure at last, and gave him the Horse with the Golden Mane, and the golden bridle. And Tsarevich Ivan mounted, found the true Elena, put her on the saddle before him, and set out on the long journey to Tsar Dolmat.

As for the Grey Wolf, he spent one day, he spent two days, then three days in Tsar Afron's palace while preparations were made for a splendid wedding. On the fourth day he asked for permission to walk on the steppe. 'Beautiful Tsarevna,' said the Tsar, 'take your serving women and your ladies in waiting, and walk wherever you please. Perhaps it will quiet your grief at parting from your father.'

And far, far away, riding with the real Tsarevna, Tsarevich Ivan suddenly remembered his promise and called out, 'Grey Wolf, I am thinking of you. Where are you?' At that instant the false princess turned into a grey wolf which ran off more swiftly than any horse. None of the Tsar's cavalry could overtake him, and he soon joined the young couple and the Horse with the Golden Mane.

With the Tsarevich riding the Grey Wolf and the Tsarevna

on the horse, they went on together to the Tsardom of Tsar
Dolmat, in whose garden hung the Firebird's cage. As they
approached the palace Tsarevich Ivan said: 'Grey Wolf, I
have one last request. Take on the shape of the Horse with
the Golden Mane, and let me deliver *you* to Tsar Dolmat in
exchange for the Firebird. Then when I am far away with the
Tsarevna you can come and join us.'

'So be it,' said the Wolf, and again he beat his paw on the
ground, whereupon he became so like the Horse with the
Golden Mane that no one could have known the difference.
Tsarevich Ivan left Elena the Beautiful outside the palace
and rode into Tsar Dolmat's presence. The Tsar received him
with great joy. He made a great banquet and there was
feasting for two days. On the third day the Tsar gave Tsarevich Ivan the Firebird in its golden cage. Ivan took it and
went back to the green lawn where he had left the Tsarevna
Elena, mounted the real Horse with the Golden Mane, set her
before him, and away they rode across three times nine
tsardoms, back towards his own country.

For two days Tsar Dolmat admired the false Horse with
the Golden Mane, and then on the third day he gave orders
for him to be saddled. Off he rode to the open steppe, but far
away Tsarevich Ivan, remembering his promise, called 'Grey
Wolf, Grey Wolf, I am thinking of you.' And at that instant
the horse turned into a wolf, who threw the Tsar and
streaked off into the distance. He soon overtook the real
Horse with the Golden Mane. The Tsarevich dismounted, got
up on Grey Wolf, and off they all went together until they

came to the forest where Grey Wolf had killed the Tsarevich's horse.

And here he stopped. 'Tsarevich Ivan,' he said, 'I have
paid for your horse many times over in loyal service. Now it
has come to an end and I must go free.'

Weeping, the Tsarevich got down from his back, and
bowed low to him. 'Do not weep,' said the Wolf, 'I may
yet come back and help you.' And he bounded off into a
thicket.

Then the Tsarevich mounted behind the Tsarevna, who
was still holding the Firebird in its cage, and off they rode
again. At last they reached the green plain with the great
stone where the three ways met, and being very tired they
got off the horse and lay down to sleep.

Now this was near the spot where the two older brothers,
Tsarevich Dimitri and Tsarevich Vassily, had been idling
away their time. But they had at last grown bored and had
decided to go back to their father even though it meant
returning empty-handed. Seeing their brother lying there
asleep, not only with the Firebird, but with a golden-maned
horse and a beautiful princess, they were maddened with
envy. Tsarevich Dimitri took his sword, killed Ivan, and
hacked him into pieces.

The Tsarevna, waking, was appalled when she saw what
they had done. Through her tears she said: 'What sort of
cowards are you? Brave knights might have challenged
him to fight. Instead of that you kill him while he is
asleep.'

But Tsarevich Vassily put the point of his sword to her breast and said: 'Listen, Elena the Beautiful. You are now at our mercy. We shall bring you to our father, Tsar Demyan, and you must tell him that it was we who found the Firebird and won both you and the Horse with the Golden Mane. If you don't swear now to this we shall put you to death.' And the Tsarevna, beside herself with fear, promised to do as they said.

So the two young men cast lots to divide up the booty. Tsarevich Vassily won Elena, and Tsarevich Dimitri took the Firebird and the Horse with the Golden Mane, and they rode back to their father's palace.

Tsar Demyan was overjoyed to see them. He gave Tsarevich Dimitri half the tsardom, since he had brought the Firebird, and he made a festival which lasted a whole month, at the end of which Tsarevich Vassily was to marry Elena the Beautiful.

Meanwhile the body of Tsarevich Ivan, cut into many pieces, lay on the green plain for thirty days. And on the thirty-first day the Grey Wolf happened to pass that way. He recognized his friend's body at once, and as he sat there grieving, a she-crow with two fledglings flew down and would have eaten the flesh. The Wolf leapt up and sprang on one of the young birds.

Then the mother Crow cried out, from a safe distance: 'O Grey Wolf, wolf's son, spare my child who has done you no harm!'

And the Grey Wolf answered: 'Listen, Crow, crow's

daughter. You can do one thing for me to save your child. I have heard that across three times nine countries, in the thirtieth tsardom, there are two springs in a place so hidden that only a bird can reach them. One is the water of death, the other the water of life. If you bring me a bottle of each your fledgling will be returned to you. If you fail I will tear it in pieces.'

The Crow flew off and the Wolf waited. He waited two days, he waited three days, and on the fourth the Crow came back with two little bottles in her beak.

The Grey Wolf tore the fledgling into pieces. He sprinkled these with the water of death, and they instantly grew together. Then he sprinkled the dead body with the water of life and the fledgling shook itself and flew away with its mother. The Grey Wolf did the same for the Tsarevich, first sprinkling the water of death, and then the water of life. And the young man sat up and stretched himself and said: 'I must have slept for a long time!'

'You would have slept for ever, Tsarevich Ivan, if it had not been for me,' said the Grey Wolf. Then he told him how his wicked brothers had killed him and stolen not only the beautiful Tsarevna but the Firebird and the Horse with the Golden Mane as well. 'Make haste,' he ended, 'for Tsarevich Vassily is to marry the Tsarevna Elena today.'

So Ivan climbed on the Wolf's back and off they sped together. They soon reached Tsar Demyan's palace. Here the Grey Wolf stopped and said: 'This is the last service I shall perform for you, Tsarevich Ivan. We have been through many dangers together; remember our journeys sometimes.'

And the Tsarevich, weeping, bowed to him three times, brushing the ground with his hand. Then he strode in through the gates, and there in the banqueting hall he found all the company seated at table for the wedding feast. As soon as Elena the Beautiful saw him she sprang up and kissed him saying: 'This is my true love, this is the man who shall marry me, and not the evil wretch beside me!'

Then she told Tsar Demyan the story of how the Tsarevich Ivan had won her, and of the wickedness of his two elder sons. The Tsar's anger was like a great river in a storm, and he commanded that the Tsareviches Dimitri and Vassily should be thrown into prison. And that day Tsarevich Ivan was married to Elena the Beautiful. The feasting lasted until there was no one in the tsardom who was hungry or thirsty, and Tsarevich Ivan lived with the beautiful Elena in peace and happiness for many years.

Сестрица Аленушка и Братецъ Иванушка.

SISTER ALENUSHKA AND
HER BROTHER IVANUSHKA

ONCE there were two children. The girl was called Elena and the boy was Ivan, but their parents lovingly called them Alenuskha and Ivanushka. When these parents died the children were all alone in the wide world, and they left their village and set out to walk – they did not know where, and they did not care, as long as the two of them were together.

One day they were travelling over a broad plain. It was high summer; the sun was burning the grass, and making the sandy ground almost too hot for their bare feet. It was beating on their heads and making their throats dry. They had been walking since early morning, and by noon the heat was so fierce that it was difficult to put one foot in front of another.

'Oh sister,' said Ivanushka, 'I am so thirsty.'

'Wait, little brother,' said Alenushka. 'Soon we must come to a well.'

They went on and on, but there was no sign of a well. Then Ivanushka saw the hoofprint of a cow in the path, and it was full of water which to his longing eyes looked as fresh and inviting as if it had been the clearest spring. 'I can drink from that!' he called joyfully to his sister.

'No, brother,' said Alenushka, pulling him back. 'If you do that you will turn into a calf. Just be patient a little longer.'

So on they stumbled, and then Ivanushka ran forward. He could see water glinting in the sun and this time it lay in a horse's hoofmark. 'No!' cried Alenushka, holding him tightly by the sleeve. 'You mustn't drink from that – you'll turn into a foal! Come along and don't look at it.'

Reluctantly Ivanushka trailed along behind her, able to think of nothing but his terrible thirst. Then he saw a footprint that his sister had not noticed. It was tiny, divided in the middle – a goat's hoofmark – but in it was a drop of

sparkling water. He said nothing to Alenushka who was plodding on in front, but knelt down, scooped up the water and drank it.

Instantly he turned into a little goat. Alenushka turned round when she heard bleating, and a kid ran up to her. She burst into tears, and sitting in the shade of a hayrick, wept and wept. The little goat at first stood gravely beside her, and then, unable to help itself, started jumping merrily.

Presently a rich merchant came riding past. He was surprised to see a beautiful girl weeping, and a kid leaping about near her. He asked her what her trouble was, and when she told him he said: 'That is a strange story, and one that is hard to believe. But come with me and marry me. The kid shall come too and you need never be parted.'

She picked up the kid and held him tight, then the merchant put her on his horse in front of him, and rode across the plain to his house. There he made a great feast and married Alenushka. They lived happily together and the little kid was always there with them. It never grew any bigger, but frisked and played, and followed Alenushka wherever she went.

Then one day the merchant had to leave his young wife and set out on a long journey. Alenushka, who loved him dearly and had never till now been parted from him, drooped and pined in his absence. Now there was a wicked witch who had long envied Alenushka and hated her for her good fortune. She came to her, and putting on a smiling face said: 'My dear, I am sorry to see you so low. Why, you are in danger of losing those good looks which won you such a fine husband! He will be back soon and then what will he say when he finds you so thin and pale? What you need is a course of sea bathing. I can promise you that if you will bathe where I say you will regain your beauty.'

Alenushka allowed herself to be led to the sea-shore. As she stepped out into the water the witch sprang behind her, pushed her down, and fastened a heavy stone round her neck. Then she dressed herself in Alenushka's clothes and turned herself into her likeness. Only the little kid, who was never far from Alenushka, had seen what had happened.

The merchant came home soon afterwards, and rejoiced to see his young wife so blooming and rosy. But the kid was strangely subdued. Instead of jumping and playing it moped and would not eat. And it was for ever wandering down to the shore and standing there, bleating. The witch knew well what the reason for this was, and she gave orders that it should be killed. She told the servants in the kitchen to sharpen their knives and to heat cauldrons of water. Then she said to the merchant: 'My dear, the kid has become a nuisance and I should be glad to see the back of it. I think the time has come to make it into a tasty stew.'

The merchant was astonished, for he knew how much his wife had loved the little creature. 'How fickle you women are,' he remarked. 'Once nothing was too good for the animal; now you want to cut its throat. Well, have it your own way.'

The kid ran away when a servant came to fetch it. It had

heard the knives being sharpened and had seen the wood
being brought in for the fire and knew what the witch was
planning. It reached the sea-shore, and the servant who had
followed it was astonished to hear it singing.

> 'Alenushka, little sister,
> They are going to slaughter me.
> They are bringing wood in faggots,
> They are heating up their saucepans,
> They are sharpening up their knives.'

And from below the water a voice came floating:

> 'Ivanushka, O my brother,
> A stone hangs heavy from my throat,

> Silken weed grows through my fingers,
> Yellow sand weighs down my breast.'

The servant marvelled and went back to fetch the merchant so he too could hear the miracle of the kid singing and the sweet voice answering it. When they came the kid was still standing by the sea. They could see it weeping, and again it sang.

> 'Alenushka, little sister,
> They mean to slaughter me.
> The wood is piled in faggots,
> The fire is burning bright,
> The cauldrons boil with water,
> They are sharpening up their knives.
> Swim out, swim out and save me!'

Then came a voice from under the waves:

> 'Ivanushka, little brother,
> A heavy stone is round my throat.
> Silken weed clings round my fingers,
> Yellow sand lies on my breast.'

The merchant sent for men with nets and they dragged the sea. At first the nets were pulled in empty, but then they brought silk ones, and there was Alenushka, lying in the net as though she were asleep. The merchant himself untied the stone from her neck, and they washed her in fresh water and dressed her in white clothes. Thereupon she awoke, sprang up and put her arms round the kid's neck. He immediately became her little brother, just as he had been before he drank out of the goat's hoofprint. Then they all went back to the merchant's house to live happily. As for the old witch, she was burnt in the fires she had prepared for the kid, and her ashes were scattered for the winds to blow over the plain.

И. Б. 1902.

БѣлаꙖ Уточка .

THE WHITE DUCK

O NCE, a long time ago, in a country far away over the seas and the mountains, a great tsar married a beautiful princess. But the rejoicings had scarcely finished before the

Tsar had to depart with his army and his ships for a distant part of his realm, leaving his weeping young bride. Her husband tried to comfort her, and gave her advice about how she should behave in his absence. She should never leave the palace, he said, never talk to strangers, and especially be on her guard against wicked women who might fill her ears with evil talk.

The young Tsarina sobbed, and promised to do all that he said. Then when he had gone she shut herself up with her ladies and sat with them spinning and weaving, and thinking about her husband. She was, as you might expect, often lonely, and time lay heavy on her hands. So that one day, when she saw an old woman hobbling around outside in the garden, she opened the window and greeted her.

'But why are you looking so sad, Tsarina?' asked the old woman. 'You should not be moping indoors on a day like this – it won't bring your royal husband back any sooner. Why not come into the garden and walk among the trees and the flowers?'

For a long time the Tsarina held back, remembering all her husband's words of warning and her own promises. Then at last she thought: 'What harm can it possibly do to step out into the fresh air and to feel the sun and the wind on my face again? It isn't natural in the summer to stay cooped up inside day after day.'

So she ran down into the garden. But the old woman leaning on her stick was really a wicked witch who envied the young Tsarina her good fortune. She spoke flattering words

and led her further and further from the palace until they reached a stream, running between steep banks and shaded by trees. 'Why not go down into the water and bathe?' said the witch artfully. 'It is a scorching day, and the stream is clear and cool.'

The Tsarina hesitated, but then the water looked so inviting that she threw off her robes and stepped in. As her feet touched the stones of the stream-bed she felt a blow on her shoulders and the witch pushed her into the deep water, calling 'Swim, little duck!' And the Tsar's young bride turned into a white duck. The witch, cackling with glee, picked up the Tsarina's robes, put them on, and turned herself into the Tsarina. Then she went back to the palace and sat down to wait for the Tsar's return.

One day soon afterwards the fleet returned, bringing the victorious Tsar and his soldiers. There was a tramp of horses' hooves, the dogs barked at the gates, and the false Tsarina ran out to greet her husband. He took her in his arms, never guessing that she was not his own dear wife, but an imposter.

As for the White Duck, she swam up and down the stream, and laid three eggs. Out of these a few days later came three fledglings – two little ducks and a drake. They grew quickly, and being bold used to stray further and further from the stream, in spite of their mother's warnings.

One day they wandered off even further than usual, and made their way to the courtyard of the palace. The witch at once recognized them and enticed them inside. She fed them, gave them a soft cushion to sleep on, and then went down to the palace kitchens. Here she ordered the servants to sharpen the knives, to make a great fire, and to boil a cauldron of water.

Meanwhile the two little ducklings had fallen asleep, and the young drake covered them with his wings to keep them warm. He alone stayed awake. In the middle of the night the witch came to the door and called: 'Little ones, are you asleep?'

And the little drake answered:

> 'We cannot sleep, we wake and weep,
> The villains mean to kill us.
> Sharp is the knife to take our life,
> The fire is hot, now boils the pot.
> All fled is sleep, we wake and weep.'

'They are not asleep yet,' muttered the witch, and went back to the kitchen. Here she paced up and down, and then returned to the ducklings. 'Are you awake, my pretties?' she called through the door.

But the little drake replied as before:

> 'We wake and weep, we do not sleep.
> There are villains out to kill us.
> The fire is hot, they boil a pot,
> They wield a knife to take our life.
> How can we sleep? We wake and weep.'

'Still the same voice?' said the witch, and she went in to see for herself. She saw the two ducklings asleep, and the eyes of the little drake just closing, and she took the knife she was carrying and killed them all.

The next day the White Duck could not find her children. Distraught, she wandered up and down the banks of the stream calling them. Then, certain that evil must have befallen them, she flew to the palace. There in the courtyard she saw their bodies laid out. She threw herself on them, and covering them with her wings cried:

> 'Alas, alas, my little loves!
> Alas, alas, my three dear doves!
> I brought you up with grief and pain,
> And now I see you lie there slain.
> I loved and watched you day and night,
> You were my joy, my sole delight.'

Inside the palace the Tsar could hear her laments, and said to his wife: 'Listen to that duck! What a strange thing it is!'

The witch answered: 'What is odd about a duck's quacking?' And she ordered the servants to chase it off. But however much they ran up and down and shouted, the duck always came back to where her children lay, crying:

> 'My loves, my loves, my little loves!
> O woe is me, my turtle doves!
> A wicked witch has killed you all,

The same false queen has me in thrall,
Changed me from a happy wife,
To a duck for all my life.'

This time the Tsar went after the duck himself, and she came down into his hands. He took her by the wing, but the witch turned her into a spindle. The spindle whispered: 'Break me in two pieces.' Bracing himself he did this, and then the piece in his right hand said: 'Throw me behind you, and the other piece before you, and say "Rise behind me, white birch; stand before me, lovely maid."' The false Tsarina rushed forward to try to snatch the pieces, but she was too late. There stood the birch tree behind the Tsar, and his own true wife in front of him.

Then from the birch tree fluttered down a magpie with a phial of the water of life in its beak. The Tsarina sprinkled the dead ducklings with the water and three beautiful children stood up, and then came running over to greet their father.

As for the witch, the Tsar ordered that her hands and feet should be tied to the tails of four horses which were whipped into a gallop across a field. Where a leg came off, a poker stood in the ground, rakes came where the arms lay, and a bush for her head. Then the winds came and blew all memory of her away, and the Tsar and the Tsarina and their children lived happily for ever.

Перышко
Финиста Ясна-Сокола.

THE FEATHER OF FINIST
THE FALCON

THERE was once a merchant whose wife had died, leaving him with three daughters. The two older girls were hard-faced, hard of heart and vain, but the youngest, who thought nothing of her looks, was beautiful, as well as kind and good and an excellent housekeeper.

One day as the merchant was setting out to trade his goods at a great fair, he called to his daughters and asked what gifts they would like him to bring back. The eldest demanded a piece of rich brocade for a gown, and the second girl wanted fine stuff to make a shawl. But the youngest said dreamily:

'Little father, just bring me a scarlet flower to put in my window.'

When the merchant came back he brought the brocade and the shawl, but had forgotten all about the flower. 'It doesn't matter, little father,' said the girl. 'Another time will do.' And he promised that next time he visited the fair he would certainly bring her what she asked for. Meanwhile the two elder sisters, sewing their fine materials, laughed at her for being a simpleton.

Time passed, and again the merchant was on the point of leaving for the fair when he asked his daughters what he should bring back for them. The eldest wanted a gold chain, her sister a pair of golden earrings, but the youngest still only asked for her scarlet flower.

Their father came back with the jewellery, but once again he was without the flower. 'Never mind, little father,' said the girl as he apologized. 'Perhaps next time I shall be luckier.'

So the third time the merchant went to the fair he resolved that he must not come back without the flower his youngest child was so patiently waiting for. It was not difficult to find the satin shoes and the silken petticoat that the two elder girls had demanded, but he searched in vain for the flower. There were plenty that were white or pink, yellow or blue, but not a single scarlet blossom, and he drove back sorrowfully, dreading to disappoint her a third time.

Then, as he neared home, he overtook a little old man whom he had never seen before. This strange being had a

hooked nose, one eye and a face covered with a golden beard like moss, and he carried a box on his back. There was something curious about this box, and the merchant stopped to ask about it.

'There is a scarlet flower in that box,' the old man told him. 'I am keeping it to give to the maiden who is to marry my son, Finist the Falcon.'

'A scarlet flower!' said the merchant eagerly. 'Please sell it to me. I'll give you a good price, and with that you can buy something more suitable for a wedding present.'

'No,' said the old man. 'With it goes the love of my son, and I have sworn to give it only to his bride.'

The merchant tried to barter with him, but it was useless. Then at last the old man said: 'You can have the flower on one condition only: that your girl promises to marry my son, Finist the Falcon.'

The merchant hesitated, but then thought of the girl who had waited so long for her flower. 'Very well,' he said. 'Give it to me, and if my child will take your son, then he shall have her.'

'Never fear,' said the old man, 'there is no girl in the world who would refuse my son.' He handed over the box, and vanished.

The merchant hurried home. He handed the two elder daughters their gifts, and turned to the youngest. 'This time I have found you what you asked for,' he said, 'but I don't know at all whether I have done the right thing. There was a strange old man who only let me have it if I promised that in return you should marry his son, Finist the Falcon.'

'You have brought me my heart's desire,' said the girl, 'and if Finist the Falcon should come to woo me, then I shall wed him.' And she took the scarlet flower lovingly, and held it close.

That night she locked herself into her room in the attic, and put the flower on the window-sill. She was standing there admiring it and looking out at the dark sky when there was a sound of rushing wings, and in through the window came flying a magnificent falcon with bright feathers. It landed on the floor, and instantly turned into a young prince, more handsome than any man she had ever seen. She was frightened at first, but he was so kind and gentle that she began to talk to him as if she had known him all her life, and the night passed away like a dream. At daybreak the prince said to her: 'Every evening, when you put the scarlet flower in the window, I will come to you. But now, when I turn into a falcon, take one feather from my wing. If you are in need of anything, go to the porch and wave it on your right side and ask for what you want. Then, when you no longer have any need of the gift, wave the feather on your left side.' Then he was gone and where he had been standing there was now a falcon. As it flew past her, she plucked a feather from its wing.

The next day was Sunday. The two older sisters dressed themselves in their new finery, telling the young one scornfully that she had better not come to church with them, her clothes were too shabby. 'Never mind,' said the young one, 'I can pray as well at home.' And she sat at her attic window,

watching the people pass by. When the street was empty she went to the porch and waved the feather on her right side. Instantly a carriage appeared with splendid horses and a coachman and footmen in gold livery. What was more, there was a gown embroidered with precious stones. She dressed herself in it, stepped into the carriage and drove away to church. Everyone turned round as she walked in, and though her sisters saw her they did not recognize in this splendid lady the shabby girl they had left at home.

As the service was nearing the end she rose, walked to the carriage and drove swiftly back. Once home, she took off her jewel-encrusted head-dress and the gown, and put on her own poor clothes. Then she waved the feather on her left side, and all the gorgeous trappings vanished as if they had never been.

Her sisters came back full of wonder at what they had seen. 'It must have been a princess at church today. Her clothes! They would have cost a king's ransom!' Then they looked at the girl in amazement; she had changed so hurriedly that she had forgotten to take a diamond pin out of her hair. 'Where on earth did you get that jewel?' they cried. They would have snatched it from her but she fled to her attic and hid the pin in the heart of the scarlet flower, and though they ransacked the room they could not find it anywhere. The sisters went to their father. 'Sir, our young sister has a secret lover who gives her jewels,' they told him. But he told them they were spiteful and envious, and he would not listen.

That evening the girl again put the flower on her window-sill. Instantly the falcon came flying in and turned into a prince, and a second night went past as though it was only a moment. But this time the sisters were listening at the attic door and they heard the murmur of voices. They rushed to their father, and told him, but he scolded them for tale-bearing and sent them away. This did not stop them from spying, however, and night after night they crouched at the keyhole, and heard their sister talking lovingly to someone within. But in the morning when she unlocked the door they could see there was no one there.

At last they devised a plan. They prepared a drink of sweet wine into which they had dropped a sleeping potion and persuaded their sister to drink it. She fell asleep at once, and they laid her on her bed, fastened open knives and sharp needles on the window-sill, and bolted the window. When darkness came, Finist the Falcon came flying to his love. The needles pierced his breast and the knives cut his brilliant wings, and though he beat against the window it remained closed. 'You have ceased to love me,' he called. 'So be it, you shall never see me again, unless first you journey through three times nine lands to the thirtieth tsardom, wear out three pairs of iron shoes in your search, break three iron staves, and gnaw away three church-loaves of stone!'

Through her drugged sleep the girl heard these bitter words, but she could not open her eyes. In the morning when she woke she saw how the window had been barred with knives and needles and she saw the blood. It was then that

she realized what had happened and she wept. And though she waved her feather and cried 'Come, my own Finist', no falcon came; the charm was broken.

Then she remembered the words she heard through her sleep. Without telling anyone she went to a blacksmith and asked him to make her three pairs of iron shoes and three iron staves, and with these and three church-loaves of stone, she set out. She walked and she walked; the telling is easy but the journey is long. She wore through one pair of iron shoes, and broke one of the iron staves to pieces, and had gnawed away one of the stone loaves, when, in the middle of a dark forest, she came to a clearing where there was a little hut. And on its step sat a sour-faced old woman.

'Oh grandmother,' said the girl, 'take pity on me! Give me shelter just for this night. I am searching for Finist the Falcon who has flown away from me.'

'He is a relative of mine,' said the old woman, 'but you will have to go a long way to find him. Come in and rest. The morning is wiser than the evening.'

She took the girl into the hut and gave her food and drink, and a bed for the night, and in the morning she woke her. 'Finist the Falcon is now in the fiftieth tsardom of the eightieth land from here. He has proposed marriage to a tsar's daughter, but if you walk fast you may get there in time for the wedding feast. Take this silver spindle; you will find it spins a golden thread and you can give that to the tsar's daughter as a wedding gift. Go now with God across three times nine tsardoms until you come to the house of a second cousin of mine. If you speak to her politely she may help you, though I warn you she is even worse-tempered than me.'

So the girl set out on her journey, across green steppe and through barren wilderness. At last, when a second pair of iron shoes were worn through, a second staff broken, and second stone loaf nibbled away, she came to a little hut on the edge of a swamp, and there she saw a cross-faced old woman sitting on the step.

'I am searching for my dear love, Finist the Falcon,' said the girl. 'And I am so weary.'

'Then come in and rest,' said the old woman. 'For you will have to walk many versts further to find him. He is to marry a tsar's daughter, and today is her last maiden feast.'

The next morning she handed the girl a golden hammer and ten little diamond nails. 'Take these,' she said. 'The hammer will drive in the nails of its own accord. You might like to give this toy to Finist's bride. Now, be off with you. Make your way to my fourth cousin who lives across three times nine lands, beside a deep river. She is even more cross-grained than I am, but speak to her fair and she may help you.'

When the girl had worn out her third pair of shoes, broken her third staff and eaten the last church-loaf, she came at last to the river, and saw the little hut with an old woman outside who was uglier and sourer than the other two put together. 'Oh grandmother, do help me,' she called. 'I am travelling the wide world to find my dear Finist the Falcon. My cruel sisters wounded him and drove him from me.'

'He is not so very far away,' the old woman said. 'But come in and rest; you will feel stronger in the morning.' And when she woke her next day she said: 'Finist the Falcon is in the next tsardom from here, in a palace beside the sea, and three days from now he is to marry the Tsar's daughter. Go now with God, and take this golden saucer and this diamond ball. If you put the ball on the plate it will roll. You could give it to the bride if you wished.'

The girl thanked the old woman and started off again. Soon after noon she came to the sea, and there high on a cliff she could see a palace of white stone whose turrets and domes glowed golden in the sun. On the shore a servant was dipping a piece of cloth in the sea and rubbing and scrubbing it. The girl asked why she was taking so much trouble.

'It is Finist the Falcon's shirt,' the servant answered. 'He is to marry my mistress in three days, but the shirt is so badly stained with blood that I cannot get it clean.' The girl knew that it must be the shirt that Finist was wearing when he was so sorely wounded by the knives, and she took it and wept. And miraculously her tears washed every spot of blood away, and the shirt became as white as snow.

Wondering, the servant took the shirt back to the Tsar's daughter, who marvelled too, and said she would like to see the girl whose tears could wipe out stains. So calling her attendants she went out to the sea-shore. She found the girl still weeping and gazing out over the sea.

'What makes you grieve like this?' she asked.

'It is because I so long to see Finist the Falcon,' the girl replied.

The Tsar's daughter tossed her head. 'Is that all! Go to the palace kitchen; you can serve at table and you may be able to catch a glimpse of him there.'

So when Finist the Falcon sat down at dinner it was the merchant's daughter who brought him his food, but he was in low spirits as he thought of his lost love, and did not raise his eyes.

When the meal was over she went sadly down to the shore and took out her little silver spindle. The Tsar's daughter came by and noticed that she was spinning a thread of pure gold. 'Will you sell me that?' she asked greedily.

'I will if you will allow me to sit up for one night beside your bridegroom,' the girl answered.

The princess saw no harm in that, but took the precaution of putting an enchanted pin in the young man's hair so that he would not wake. All night through, the merchant's daughter bent over the bed, weeping over the handsome youth. 'Awake, Finist, my bright Falcon,' she cried. 'I have come to you at last!' But Finist did not stir, and in the morning she had to go back to the kitchen.

'Did you sleep well?' the princess asked her bridegroom.

'Well enough,' he answered. 'But all night I seemed to hear somebody beside me weeping and lamenting, though I couldn't rouse myself to see who it was.'

'It was just a bad dream,' she told him. 'There was no one there.'

So Finist called for his horse and went out hunting. And

when in the evening the girl waited on him at table, he was too melancholy to notice her. Sorrowfully she went down to the shore, taking with her the golden hammer and the diamond nails. As the Tsar's daughter passed her she saw how the hammer was driving in the nails all by itself, and she coveted this toy too.

'You shall have it,' said the girl, 'if you let me sit up by your bridegroom for a second night.'

And the princess agreed, though she took care to put the enchanted pin into the young man's hair before she brought the girl to his room. The merchant's daughter besought him to wake. 'Finist, my love, speak to me!' she called. 'I have travelled so wearily to find you! I have journeyed to the fiftieth tsardom of the eightieth land! I have washed the blood from your shirt with my tears!'

But Finist slept on. Next morning, when the Tsar's daughter saw him, she asked if he felt refreshed. 'My heart is heavy,' he told her. 'All night I felt there was somebody that I loved watching me and begging me to wake, but I was unable to open my eyes.'

She scoffed, and told him it was all fancy, and that he would feel better after a day's hunting. So he had his horse saddled and rode off to the open steppe.

The next day was to be the wedding day, and the merchant's daughter wept as she thought how she would be losing her bright falcon for ever. In the evening she went down to the shore again, and took out the golden plate and put the diamond ball on it. As the ball went rolling round the

plate the Tsar's daughter stopped to watch, and longed to have these for her own too.

'You can have them for the same price as before,' said the girl.

'What a fool she is!' the princess thought. She agreed gladly, and when Finist the Falcon fell asleep that night, she put the enchanted pin into his hair again, and then brought the girl into his room. Finist could hear her weeping and calling upon him. 'I have worn through the three pairs of iron shoes,' she kept telling him. 'I have broken three iron staves while trudging the weary world to find you; I have eaten three stone church-loaves, and all for you, my love, oh my love!'

But the enchanted pin stopped him from opening his eyes.

As daybreak drew near and she knew that she must soon go, the girl bent down to kiss him farewell. As she put her arms round him, she noticed the pin and pulled it out, in case it should hurt him. Instantly he opened his eyes and saw her, and realized that it was she whom he had heard crying beside him. She told him about her wicked sisters, about her labours to find him, and about the greed of the Tsar's daughter and the enchantment she had used.

Then Finist's anger was roused against the woman he had so nearly wed, and, turning into a falcon, he flew off with the merchant's daughter to his own tsardom. There he called all his princes and nobles and, when he had told them the story, asked: 'Which of these two shall I marry?'

They all shouted: 'Marry the one who has toiled over fifty lands to find you!'

And so Finist the Falcon married his own true love.

GILLIAN AVERY (1926–   ) was born in Reigate, Surrey, where she started her writing career as a journalist on the *Surrey Mirror*. Deciding that the pace of book publishing was more congenial than that of newspapers, she went to Oxford in 1950 to work for the Clarendon Press. In 1952 she married a don, Anthony Cockshut, and when they moved to Manchester she was so homesick for Oxford that she set her first novel, *The Warden's Niece* (1957), in an Oxford college in Victorian times, feeling an affinity between her own pre-war generation and the Victorian child, characterized by a 'meek acceptance of the power of the adult world'. Returning to Oxford in 1964, she continued to write novels, including *A Likely Lad*, set in Manchester, which won the *Guardian* award for children's fiction in 1971 and was successfully dramatized as a children's TV serial.

Gillian Avery is also well known as a reviewer and historian of children's literature. Her two most recent books are *Behold the Child: American Children and their Books, 1621–1922* and *The Everyman Anthology of Poetry for Children*.

IVAN BILIBIN (1876–1942) was born in Tarkhova, near St Petersburg, the son of a physician. Although he studied law and qualified as a lawyer in 1900, his heart was in drawing, for which he had a natural talent, developed by work in private art studios in Munich and St Petersburg. Commissioned in 1899 by the Department for the Production of State Documents in Moscow to illustrate a series of fairy tales, he took four years to complete the task, which convinced him that book illustration was his vocation.

In 1902 he married a fellow-artist, Maria Chambers, by whom he had two sons. He now began to design for the stage, producing sets and costumes for new productions of Rimsky-Korsakov's *Snow Maiden* in 1904 and Mussorgsky's *Boris Godunov* in 1908, and relishing the opportunity to display his fascination with Russian national dress and wooden architecture. For the rest of his life he combined work in the theatre with illustration (he always loved fairy tales), portrait and landscape painting.

He left his family in 1911 and remarried a year later, but this marriage also foundered in 1917. He then travelled to Egypt and he spent several years painting landscapes in Palestine and Syria. He married Alexandra Shchekatikhina-Pototskaya in 1923 and settled in Paris two years afterwards, passing the summers in Provence where he had bought a plot of land.

Bilibin returned to St Petersburg, now Leningrad, in 1936, when he was appointed Professor of Graphic Art at the Institute of Painting, Sculpture and Architecture. He remained there during the terrible days of the German blockade in 1941 and died early the following year.